MOUNTAIN ECSTASY

He traced the smooth arch of her neck and dipped his fingers into the hollow of her shoulder blade. She was all honey and cream. He bent his head to taste her.

"What are you doing?"

"You're cold. I'm warming you up."

"But you gave your word—"

Max pulled back from her and lost himself in the shadows of her brown eyes. "My God, Samantha," he said. "I want you so badly. So badly."

Samantha shivered. His warm sighs echoed in her ear as he ran his lips up and down her neck, making her heart flutter like the fragile wings of a hummingbird. She couldn't find the will to stop him.

"To hell with promises," he whispered. His lips grazed against her sensitive skin. "To hell with the world."

Also by Suzanne Elizabeth

When Destiny Calls
Kiley's Storm*

Available from HarperPaperbacks

*coming soon

Harper Monogram

Fan the Flame

Suzanne Elizabeth

HarperPaperbacks
A Division of HarperCollinsPublishers

If you purchased this book without a cover, you should be aware that this book is stolen property. It was reported as "unsold and destroyed" to the publisher and neither the author nor the publisher has received any payment for this "stripped book."

This is a work of fiction. The characters, incidents, and dialogues are products of the author's imagination and are not to be construed as real. Any resemblance to actual events or persons, living or dead, is entirely coincidental.

HarperPaperbacks *A Division of* HarperCollins*Publishers*
10 East 53rd Street, New York, N.Y. 10022

Copyright © 1993 by Suzanne E. Witter
All rights reserved. No part of this book may be used or reproduced in any manner whatsoever without written permission of the publisher, except in the case of brief quotations embodied in critical articles and reviews. For information address HarperCollins*Publishers*, 10 East 53rd Street, New York, N.Y. 10022.

Cover illustration by R. A. Maguire

First printing: September 1993

Printed in the United States of America

HarperPaperbacks, HarperMonogram, and colophon are trademarks of HarperCollins*Publishers*

❖ 10 9 8 7 6 5 4 3 2 1

*To Hazel and Jerry Hickman,
for giving me the courage to chase my dreams.
Thanks, Mom and Dad.*

Prologue

Washington Territory, 1880

Samantha's heart was pounding like the hooves of the mare beneath her as she galloped through the foliage tunnel toward her house. She bet they were both having a good laugh, Randy and Julia. A good laugh as they rolled around in the hay of *her* barn!

She fought the tears that were threatening to fall and wondered how this could all be happening to her again.

Reverend Parker could not be wrong. He was too kind and too intelligent to make such an accusation without good cause. When he'd called her into his office at the church that morning she'd assumed it was to discuss her and Randy Duncan's upcoming wedding. But instead the sympathetic man had informed her that Randy was being unfaithful to her, and with Julia Thorn no less—the fastest woman this side of a steam locomotive.

At first Samantha had doubted Reverend Parker's theory. What were the chances of something like this happening to her twice? So, hoping to prove the man wrong, she'd jumped on her horse and headed straight for Randy's farm. Randy hadn't been home all afternoon. His brother was under the impression he was spending the day with Samantha, and then a stop at the Thorns' house revealed that Mrs. Thorn thought Julia would also be with Samantha all afternoon.

At that point Samantha could come to only one heartbreaking conclusion. Randy knew she was planning on being at the church all day, making arrangements for their wedding, and he knew her father spent Wednesdays helping Amos Clemens with his weekly inventory at the mercantile. The James farm would therefore be deserted all afternoon, and Randy was obviously using it for his and Julia's rendezvous!

Pulling her mare up short in front of her house, Samantha slipped from the saddle. She looked through a blur of tears at the empty yard, and a glimmer of hope that maybe the Reverend had indeed been wrong lit her heart. Maybe this time things would turn out differently.

Despite her experience with philandering men, she had always trusted Randy and believed him each time he'd sworn to her how much he loved her. When his cowhand job had taken him on a four-month drive into Colorado she'd never once doubted his loyalty. She'd waited patiently for him to come home, believing he was longing for her just as she was for him.

She'd thought Randy was completely unlike Ty Orbison, who, despite his frequent claims of undying love, had stared at, flirted with, and bedded down anything in a skirt. Randy, in the two months of their engagement, had never given Samantha any reason to doubt his sincerity. How fair was she being now, judging him on the word of another?

Her gaze drifted toward the closed door of the barn. They could be in there, wrapped in each other's arms, laughing at her gullibility. But if she so much as peeked through a dusty window, she would be betraying the trust that was so important in their relationship.

She stood in the yard, not sure what to do, until a stream of giggles drifted out from the direction of the barn. A knot tightened in the pit of her stomach. They were in there, all right. And everything Randy Duncan had ever said to her had been a lie.

She ran up the steps to her house and burst through the front door. In three great strides she reached the rock fireplace and yanked the long shotgun off the wall above the mantel. She could feel her heart harden in her chest, much like it had two years before. Only this time, she vowed, it would never again be softened by the pretty words of a man. True love, she told herself, was only a myth.

She hurried back out the door, clenching the shotgun under her arm. She paused before the barn door, knowing that if she didn't calm herself down, she was going to put a barrel of buckshot in both of them. Randy Duncan wasn't worth hanging for. She took a deep breath and pulled open the door.

Dust particles danced around the room in the faint sunlight streaming in from the loft window above. Samantha released the door, tears of rage beginning to stream down her cheeks. The pair before her had yet to notice her presence. They were too intent on straining over each other in the middle of the barn floor. Randy's and Julia's clothes were in disarray, and Samantha didn't need a vast imagination to figure out what they were doing. They were down on all fours, breeding like a couple of wild animals!

Samantha lifted the barrel of the shotgun. "You son of a bitch!"

Randy's face shot up, and he scrambled to his feet. "H-hold on, Sam! It's not what you think!" He turned his back to her and fumbled with the buttons on his pants.

"Really?" She swung the barrel toward Julia, who let out a shriek and struggled to pull the front of her dress over her large, bare breasts. "I suppose you were just rehearsing for the church play?"

Randy tried again. "Sam, you know how much I love—"

Samantha squeezed the trigger and let a loud shot fly through the ceiling of the barn. A light spray of dust and hay showered down on them, while outside the horses whinnied and the chickens squawked in surprise. She'd seen that look before, she'd heard the apologies before, and they all came down to the same thing: lies. How could she have gotten herself into a situation like this again?

"Goddammit, Samantha! You tryin' to kill me? Put that thing down!"

He took a step toward her, and she leveled the shotgun at his chest. "You move one step closer to me and I'll blow you through the wall of this barn."

"Sam, what's gotten into you?"

"Oh, I think it's more what's gotten into Julia."

"This is so unlike you! Give me a chance to explain—"

She laughed. "I'd do that, Randy, but you see the idea of dying with a noose around my neck scares the daylights out of me. And if I let you start talking, I'm surely going to shoot you in half."

She wanted to shoot him. She wanted to blast him clean into next year. Not only him, but Ty Orbison and every other man like them. She stared at Randy's face as tears moistened her eyes. He was a handsome man, the kind who could smile and make a woman believe every word he said. Even now, when he'd been caught red-handed, his brown eyes looked almost persuasive.

She reached behind her and shoved open the barn door. "Get out! Both of you!"

When they were standing in the yard, Randy tried to speak again, but she poked him in the stomach with the barrel of the shotgun. "The engagement's off. Now get the hell off my property!"

Randy didn't appear inclined to move. "All right, Sam, if that's the way you feel. But what about my ring?"

She looked down at the tiny diamond glittering on the third finger of her left hand. "Mr. Tucker will give me a fair price for it. I could use a few new dresses and a pair of shoes."

"You're makin' a mistake, Samantha James."

"No, Randy, I'm just correcting one."

He took Julia by the arm and led her around to the back of the barn. A few seconds later they galloped off on their horses and disappeared down the road.

Samantha sank to the ground. She'd never get the image of the two of them, together on the barn floor, out of her mind. Tears flooded her vision.

"I should have shot him."

1

Billings, Montana Territory

In his room above the One Shot Saloon, U.S. Marshal Max Barrett sat on a frayed brocade couch, waiting for his prey. His sharp eyes stared out the grimy window and fixed on the "cat" house across the street. His only movement was the twitch of his moustache as the dust floating around him tickled his nose.

Narrowing his eyes, he leaned forward for a better look at the man entering Mollie's. He'd known that all he had to do was wait long enough and John Strickland would come to him. On Strickland's last train robbery every person in the first-class car had been killed. He hadn't bothered to take any female companionship with him, and without a woman Max knew the man was bound to show up at one of the local bordellos.

Max lifted his colt .45 out of its holster and checked the cylinder. A Strickland was no one to take chances with. Three dead deputy marshals had already learned that the hard way.

He rose from the couch and left the room, his spurless boots thudding softly on the brown carpet, which was a perfect shade for hiding dirt. He descended the stairs to the saloon below and moved through a crowd of jostling men who didn't spare him a glance. He'd long ago given up the dangerous practice of wearing his badge on the outside of his clothes. Then he pushed open the saloon doors and went outside into the cool night air.

He focused his mind on his job, which at times like this, when he was about to bring down one of the most vicious men of the decade, almost seemed satisfying.

He crossed the street and walked through the open glass doors of Mollie's into a dramatic entryway dominated by a large crystal chandelier. He did a quick check of the room and found no one in the place had the distinguishing burly size or the bushy carrot-colored hair of a Strickland.

"Well, howdy, stranger. You must be new in town."

Max looked down at the small woman. "You Mollie?"

"Why, yes I am, sugar." She pressed her well-displayed breasts against his arm. "What can I do for ya?"

It had been a while for Max, and any other time

he might have been interested. But business had to come first. He flipped back the edge of his vest and flashed his badge. "You can tell me which room John Strickland's in."

The woman raised her thin eyebrows but said nothing.

Max laughed. "Look, lady. It's fine with me if I have to shoot locks and break down doors to find this fella. I just thought I'd spare you the expense." He moved past her toward the staircase, knowing she'd stop him.

"Wait." After glancing around for listeners, she said softly and quickly, "Room four."

He tugged at the brim of his hat. "Much obliged." Then he went up the stairs.

He looked up and down the hallway before setting foot on the plush Oriental carpeting of the second floor. He went left, watching each door, until he came to room four at the end of the hall.

He listened and then smiled at the sound of a bed squeaking. He opened the door and slipped quietly inside the room to wait for the pumping red-headed man to be done with his business.

The whore saw him first from her place beneath the large man. A small exclamation of curses sprang from her smeared red lips.

"John Strickland? You're under arrest."

Moving with surprising speed, Strickland vaulted from the bed. He was still wearing his mud-splattered boots and his face was turning red and blotchy with rage. "Is this what you boys call fightin' fair? Sneakin' up on a man and puttin' a pistol in his back when he's screwin'?"

"Ain't fair I'm after, John. Just justice. You best put your clothes on unless you'd like to be paraded through town buck naked.

"And don't make any sudden moves," Max warned as Strickland bent to retrieve his pants from the floor. "I wouldn't want to have to shoot off anything important."

Strickland jammed his legs into his pants, cursing God for inventing the U.S. Marshal. He slipped on his shirt, crammed the tails into his pants, and buttoned up his fly.

All the while the whore complained loudly from the bed. "You don't think you can just slip in here and watch without payin' me somethin', do ya?"

Max gave her a cold glare, and she sprang from the bed at him.

That instant was all Strickland needed, and Max knew it before the man even made his move. The foresight did the lawman little good, however, as Strickland gave the whore a shove and she came tumbling toward Max. Then Strickland did a one-handed leap out the window and onto the roof of the nearby mercantile.

"Damn!"

Max untangled the woman from him and followed his prisoner out the window. He searched the roof and then slid down a pillar to the street below. He steadied his gun and stood perfectly still, listening, and one by one singled out each sound until he found the one he wanted: hastily retreating, spurred boots.

He turned and rushed down the alley behind him. Strickland was heading down Lane Street, which intersected with Grant Avenue. If Max was fast enough, he could beat him to the intersection.

Max rounded the corner onto Lane just as his man burst around the corner from the other direction. Strickland had a gun in his hand and it was aimed directly at Max's chest. Max fired without second thought, and the big man crumbled to the ground in a heap, the bright full moon shining down on his lifeless face.

The marshal nudged the dead man with his boot and then reholstered his gun. He liked to bring his men in alive, but this particular death he didn't mind. It would save the country the expense of a hanging and send Strickland to hell that much quicker.

He tipped his hat back and stared up at the stars, feeling a weariness seep through him. By this time next week he'd be sleeping in a soft bed, eating a home-cooked meal, and enjoying the company of a good friend.

He'd been asked to do a favor for an old associate, and he sure as hell needed the diversion.

He could feel exhaustion weakening his legs. And a tired lawman usually meant a dead lawman.

He picked up Strickland's gun and began walking toward the local sheriff's office.

2

Samantha stood with Melissa Cauldwell on the boardwalk in front of Amos's Mercantile, the busy sounds of Main Street all around them. Melissa was telling Samantha the latest episode in the month-long courtship of Randy Duncan and Julia Thorn, and Samantha was listening patiently, wishing she had the courage to look Melissa square in the eye and tell her how painful it was for her to hear any news on the subject. Not so much a pain to the heart, but a pain to her still stinging pride. The whole town had heard of the incident not a day after its occurrence, and the overblown sympathy and whispered snickers had all but driven Samantha crazy.

" . . . and then Julia socked him square in the nose," Melissa was saying.

"I wish I'd socked him square in the nose."

"Once a straying man always a straying man. Randy messing with Yolanda Fields serves Julia right. He asked me about you, you know."

"Did he," Samantha's said in a monotone.

"I told him if he wanted to know how you were doing he could ask you himself, if he had the courage."

That statement got a smile out of Samantha. Not only had the whole town heard of the incident at the barn, they'd also heard about how Samantha James had run the groping pair off with a loaded shotgun.

"Anyway, after a few cups of the Brumfords' punch at the party, chances are he'll find the courage to approach you, Sam, so you best be prepared. He was surprised when I told him you were leaving town. You should write a speech or something. Have you decided what you're going to wear yet?"

Samantha grimaced. Here it was, the moment she'd been dreading ever since the Reverend Parker and his wife had come up with the idea for a going-away party for her. "I, uh, don't think I'm going."

It wasn't that she didn't appreciate the Reverend and Mrs. Parker's gesture, but the thought of attending this party only to have people hugging her and patting her hand while Randy and Julia snuggled up together in a far corner made her stomach go sour.

"But the party is in your honor! You can't disappoint the Parkers!"

"Marshal Barrett is supposed to be arriving any

day. I . . . I can't very well run off to a dance when there's company at the house."

"That's just an excuse and you know it. Why not bring the man with you?"

"I hardly think a United States Marshal would be interested in a hill-town barn dance. Besides, he and I will have a lot of planning to do before we leave. A two-week trip through the mountains is nothing to rush headlong into."

Melissa raised her dark brows. "Maybe you should have thought of that before you accepted this teaching position."

"Don't start, Mel. You know my reasons for doing this as well as I do. I can't stay here anymore. I need something new, something different in my life."

"I hope that little school in Utah knows what a treasure they're getting."

"Stop it, or we're both going to be blubbering all over the boardwalk again."

"It just makes me so mad. You're leaving—and it's all because of that snake Randy Duncan!"

"Shhh! I'm sure the whole town assumes that, but I'd rather their suspicions weren't confirmed."

Melissa sniffed. "Sorry. I don't suppose you have a hanky in that thing?" she asked, indicating Samantha's reticule.

"Of course." Samantha went to reach into the bag, but it slipped from her wrist and dropped to the ground. Before she could retrieve it a man picked it up and handed it to her.

She didn't look up at the man, she was too busy staring at his hand. It was large and strong, and tanned a deep dark brown.

"Thank you," she whispered.

"You're welcome."

His smooth voice brought her attention to his face. She glanced up and felt the color drain from her cheeks. He was tall and golden-haired, with the clearest, bluest eyes she'd ever seen. Under his long straight nose was a neat, rusty-brown moustache, and Samantha found herself wondering if that thick patch of hair was as soft as it looked.

This was a man she would have paid attention to two years ago, before Randy, before Ty. But now, instead of feeling an automatic attraction, she felt a cool chill of apprehension. Men like this, she reminded herself, could take a trusting heart and tear it to shreds.

He smiled at her, briefly, and tipped his gray hat. Samantha couldn't help watching him as he moved past her and into the mercantile.

"Now, there's a man that could steal a woman's heart," Melissa whispered in her ear. "Don't look at him too long, Sam, or your eyes will fall out."

Samantha quickly turned her back on the sight of the tall stranger, mentally checking her heart, which still felt like a rock in her chest.

"One look from those eyes and a woman would jump to do his bidding," Melissa continued.

"And he's probably well aware of it too."

"Oh, I hope he's at the party! Wouldn't it be divine to dance with that gorgeous towering man draped over you?"

"Why would a man like that be at my going-away party, Mel? And your father would shoot him if his breath so much as lifted your hair."

"Oh, that reminds me. There's a hat at the milliner's I want you to see. I just know it will look incredible with my blue organdy."

Samantha fell into step beside Melissa. Her pride allowed her to look back at the mercantile only three times.

The two spent the day shopping, picking out hats and dresses for the party Melissa had finally talked her into attending. Soon the sun began to set, and a soft warm breeze sifted through her hair, teasing her nose with the sweet scent of apple blossoms. She'd grown up in Spokane Falls, spent her whole life here. Leaving was going to be the hardest thing she'd ever done.

Samantha arrived home just before suppertime. Twilight had taken over the sky and the first faint stars were beginning to glitter. Finding the front room of the house empty, she went back to the kitchen and then froze to the wood-plank floor. Standing at the counter was the tall man with the mesmerizing eyes. She found herself struck speechless as he smiled at her. "Good evening."

"I—What are you doing in my kitchen?"

Her question had come out sounding like a

demand, and he looked a little surprised. "I believe I was invited to dinner."

Samantha heard the thump of her father's cane behind her and turned to see him limp into the room. "You didn't tell me we were having company for dinner, Daddy."

She was trying to sound calm, but her racing heart was making her voice jangly. She could almost feel the tall man's penetrating eyes boring into her back. Her shoulder blades began to itch.

"That's because I wasn't aware of the man's arrival until he knocked on the door." Ed James was looking at her oddly, no doubt wondering at her rude behavior.

"I remember you," the man said. "Didn't we meet earlier today, in front of the mercantile?"

"Yes, sir, I believe we did. If you'll excuse me I have some packages to take to my room." She thought maybe she would hide in her room until the man left. He made her nervous.

"The packages can wait until the two of you have been properly introduced. Sam, this is Marshal Barrett, your escort to Utah."

Samantha's jaw dropped open. This couldn't possibly be him! Marshal Barrett had worked with her father over ten years ago! He'd killed wild animals and slain renegade Indians. He'd roughed it out in the wilderness without food and water for days on end. No, Marshal Barrett had to be a much older man. A much more weathered, hardened, older man.

"I assumed your father told you I was coming," the marshal said.

"I told her all right. Sam, close up your mouth, you look like a dying fish."

She snapped her mouth shut but continued to stare at the marshal. "I'm sorry. I just expected . . ."

"That he'd be older than the hills like me?" Her father laughed. "Back in '70 we used to call ol' Max here 'Boy.' Remember that?"

The marshal's smile seemed a bit pained. "How could I forget?"

"'Boy, get me some coffee. Boy, roll me a cigarette.' Boy, this. Boy, that. If I recall, you flattened George Montgomery's nose one day for asking you to wipe his—"

The marshal cleared his throat. Samantha's father seemed to have forgotten that she was in the room. "Uh . . . anyway, Max was just a pup when he was assigned to my group. But he proved himself soon enough. Took a bullet in the shoulder, saving my life."

"And you took a bullet in the leg saving mine."

"Yep. I figured since you were still in one piece, while I got a bum leg for my trouble, it wouldn't hurt to ask you this little favor."

The marshal turned his eyes on Samantha. Something warm flickered in them, and she stole a desperate glance at her father. Hadn't he noticed it? Or had it only been her imagination?

"I'm happy to help you and your daughter out, Ed."

She couldn't believe this was happening. A susceptible woman like herself couldn't roam through the wilderness alone with a man like this. After one night he'd be doing a dance on her heart around the campfire.

Don't look at him too long, Sam, or your eyes will fall out.

She was supposed to talk, eat, ride . . . live with this man for half a month?

One look from those eyes and a woman would jump to do his bidding.

Both men stared at her, waiting for her to say something. "I . . . maybe I should rethink this whole situation."

Her father looked shocked. "Sam, the people of Logan are counting on you to be their new teacher."

She knew that, and deep down inside it was still what she wanted to do. But right now all she could think about was protecting her vulnerable, gullible heart from the stunning man standing in front of her.

Her father sensed her hesitation. "You're just getting cold feet now that the marshal's here, but you'll still have two more days to say your goodbyes, Sam. You've made the right decision. Besides, it's not like we'll never see each other again. Once they've got that railroad built, you and that crazy aunt of yours won't be able to keep me away from Logan with a nest of rattlers."

Samantha nodded. Her father was right. She was

only worried and upset about leaving her home. Her sudden bout of nerves had nothing to do with the incredible specimen of a man she was to be alone with, completely unchaperoned. But only if she didn't look at Marshal Barrett could she believe that.

Supper that night was a mixture of clatters and mumbles from her side of the table. She seemed to drop something everytime the marshal looked her way, and she wasn't sure whether her mounting anger should be directed at him or at herself. Whenever she began to think things couldn't possibly get worse, he'd ask her a question that either she wouldn't hear because she was staring at that darn moustache of his, or she'd answer in a cracking, barely audible voice.

By the time the meal was finished she was so tense her neck hurt. She couldn't wait to flee into the privacy of her room. As soon as the marshal set down his fork, she sprang up from her chair and gave her father a quick peck on the cheek. "Well, I'm tired. Good night, Daddy." She glanced at the marshal. "Marshal Barrett."

He smiled at her faintly and dipped his head. "Good night, Miss James. I'll see you in the morning."

Yes, he would see her in the morning, and every morning after that for the next two weeks.

She walked down the hall, fighting the urge to run to her room. Once inside, she closed the door quietly and leaned back against the solid wood. Her heart was racing. She felt like she was struggling in a pit of quicksand and couldn't find a branch to pull herself out.

The answer was simple: She wouldn't let herself succumb to this man's obvious charms. It wouldn't be like previous times, when she'd believed every word Ty and Randy had said. No matter her attraction, she would fight Marshal Barrett with everything she had. He could smile or wink or tell her he loved her a hundred times over, for all she cared, but she wasn't going to surrender.

3

Max Barrett took off his dirty clothes and left them on the bank of the Spokane River. Clenching his teeth, he stepped into the icy water and sank down until it lapped at his waist. He quickly scrubbed a week's worth of riding dust off his body and out of his hair, then rose from the water and toweled himself off in the moonlight.

He'd made a mistake.

He should have never agreed to escort Ed's daughter through the mountains, even though he owed the man his life.

Samantha James was as skittish as a wild kitten. He'd expected her to be bookish, even prudish, since she was heading for Utah to be a teacher. But, damn, if she wasn't the prettiest thing he'd seen in a long time. For the life of him, Max couldn't imagine what

Ed James had been thinking when he'd asked him to do this job. Sure, he and Ed were old friends, but, friend or not, Marshal Max Barrett was still a man. And Lord Almighty, Samantha James was all woman.

There wasn't much he could do about the situation now except mark Ed's daughter as off limits and do his best to keep his hands to himself. It was plain as day that the woman was attracted to him, though. He could see that she was fighting it every step of the way.

As he dressed in a clean shirt and pants, he decided it would be best for both him and Miss James if she changed her mind and decided to stay on in Spokane Falls. She wouldn't want a man like him, and he sure as hell didn't need any more women complicating his life. A pushy grandmother, a domineering mother, a headstrong sister, and a very determined young woman named Camille St. Clair were about all he could handle at the moment.

Maybe with a little effort on his part he could avoid this trip through the mountains and squelch the spark between him and the lovely Miss James before it had a chance to flicker to a flame.

Samantha slipped out the front door. She'd been lying in her bed for three hours, and she hadn't been able to get a wink of sleep. She had Max Barrett on the brain. What she needed to get him out of her head was a brisk walk to the river.

Halfway down the trail she saw the marshal coming her way. She could never mistake his towering height, even in the moonlight. The thought of darting into the woods crossed her mind, but, unfortunately, he had already seen her.

"Good evening, Miss James."

"Marshal." Thank God her voice hadn't trembled.

"I thought you'd gone to bed."

"I—uh—needed some air."

He peered at her through the darkness. "You're upset about the trip."

"I'm a little nervous. I think that's understandable."

"You do know, of course, that I won't let anything happen to you?"

"I'm sure you won't," she said quickly.

He smiled, and she felt warm clear to her toes. "You can't be too confident in me if this whole thing is keeping you awake at night. Or is it something else that's got you restless?"

There was an intimacy in his voice that made Samantha's cheeks flame. She was grateful for the darkness. Then he said, "Your father told me the reason you decided to head for Utah."

She clenched her jaw. "He shouldn't have said anything."

"Maybe not. But are you sure you know what you're doing? You seemed less than convinced earlier this evening."

She hated that he knew so much about her, that her father had told him all the sordid details of her silly love life. She felt embarrassed, foolish.

"Despite what my father and this whole town seem to think, Marshal, I am not being driven away by a wayward beau. I am twenty years old and should be moving on with my life."

There was a pause before he spoke again. "You still haven't gotten over this fellow, have you?"

"That's an awfully strong assumption from someone who's known me less than half a day."

"I see."

There was another pause, in which Samantha continued to grow increasingly annoyed.

He ran a hand through his damp hair. "Look, you might as well stop trying to fool yourself, Miss James, 'cause you're not fooling anybody else. You haven't gotten over this fellow. You're running. It's pretty plain."

The anger Samantha had felt that evening at supper came back in full force, and this time she knew exactly who to direct it toward. "Don't you dare stand there and presume to know what I'm thinking, Mr. Barrett, because I can assure you, you have no idea. I have made my decision regarding this teaching position, but if you'd like to back out of your agreement with my father, that is fine with me. There are plenty of men who could take your place."

He laughed softly, which had even more of an effect on her than just his smile. "There aren't many

FAN THE FLAME 27

men who could take my place, Miss James. Let's both hope you never find that out."

"Is that a threat?"

His eyes flashed at her, and she took a step back in defense. "That's a statement. Would you like to hear a threat? I made a promise to your father, and I plan to see it through to the end. The absolute end, Miss James. There will be no turning back midstride. Once we're on the trail it's all the way to Utah. So, you'd best be sure you're making the right decision before you climb up on your horse Sunday morning."

"My mind is already made up about this trip. Much like it's beginning to be made up about you."

"Really?" he said. "You know, I've been dying to hear what you think of me. In fact, it's been eating away at me in little bits and pieces all night."

"I wish you'd gather all those pieces, along with your monumental arrogance, and ride back to the cave you crawled out of!"

"Ah, you wound me. And I had expected us to become such great friends."

"What I expect is that you'll take me through the mountains—and safely—to my aunt in Logan, Utah."

"Then we have our stories straight?"

"Excuse me?"

"What I say I expect from you, and what you say you expect from me."

He was talking in circles, and she was becoming more and more exasperated. "What I say I expect from you, sir, is exactly what I mean!"

He smiled broadly. "Do you lie to everybody else as good as you lie to yourself?"

Samantha took a deep breath. "Mr. Barrett—Marshal—I don't know what you're driving at, and, frankly, I don't care to know. I think you should just head on up the trail the way you were going and we should pretend this meeting never took place."

"You mean try again in the morning?"

"Exactly." By then maybe she'd have figured a way out of this whole mess.

"So you think maybe the sun shining in our eyes might blind us into seeing each other differently?"

"One can only hope."

He moved closer to her and bent down until she felt his hot breath in her face. "I'm not a flower that opens with the sunrise, Miss James. What you see now is what you get tomorrow. And the next day, and the next. Daunting, isn't it?"

She held her ground, refusing to take a step back from him and hoping she wouldn't regret it. "Annoying is more the word—and if you kiss me, I'll scream."

"What makes you think I'm going to kiss you?" he whispered, practically into her mouth.

"Because you're a man, Mr. Barrett. And apparently worse than most."

He hovered over her, staring at her lips and breathing his warmth into her face. She didn't know what she'd do if he kissed her—screaming was an inane notion, considering they were out in the middle of nowhere. She supposed she'd curl up and die, right here at his feet. She'd wither and fade like the weak female she was turning out to be.

Just when she'd convinced herself to turn tail and run, he stepped back from her. "I'll see you in the morning, Miss James. Maybe between then and now you should think hard on what's been said here tonight."

He turned and walked up the trail before she had a chance to respond, before she had a chance to think of a response. She didn't know what to do. She couldn't spend two weeks in the middle of nowhere with this lunatic. But she couldn't back down on her determination to leave, either. And she knew she'd never be able to convince her father to find her another escort, no matter how much she begged. Max Barrett was a guaranteed safe ticket through the mountains as far as Ed James was concerned. There was just no way around it. She and Marshal Barrett were stuck with each other, whether she liked it or not.

Barrett wandered into the kitchen when Samantha was making breakfast the next morning. His hair was tousled, his shirt was buttoned wrong, and he wasn't wearing any shoes, or even socks.

To Sam's consternation, his large, wide feet had the same effect on her as did his big hands. She was losing her mind. There was no other explanation for it. Why else would the sight of a man's big, stinky feet attract her interest?

He said good morning and seated himself at the table. "It's been a long time since I've had home cooking."

Samantha picked up the frying pan, still trying to get over the man's darn feet, and walked over to the table. Her hand shook as she served him some scrambled eggs. Then she hurried back to the stove like a chased mouse.

A few moments later she heard her father's familiar thump as he came into the room. "What the hell is that?" he asked, looking at Marshal Barrett's plate.

"I think it's eggs," the marshal said.

Samantha looked down at his plate and saw, to her horror, that she'd given him a breakfast of runny mess.

"Gee, Sam, don't you think you should've cooked the eggs first?"

She snatched the plate off the table and tossed it into the sink with a clatter. She wanted to say that it served the man right for harassing her the night before, but the last thing she wanted to have to do was tell her father about their encounter.

"I'd like you to try some of our river trout before you leave, Barrett," her father said. "This ol' bum leg of mine makes the hike down there a little inconvenient, so if you wouldn't mind, I'll need you and Sam to go this afternoon and catch us some fish for supper."

"No!" Samantha said before she could stop herself.

Both men looked up at her in surprise.

"I—I mean, I've always caught the fish alone before. You know I can do it by myself, Daddy."

"Samantha, we'll need at least five big ones to feed all three of us. You can't carry that much trout up the hill."

"Then I'll make two trips." She was sounding like the fool she was fast becoming, but she didn't care. She was willing to do just about anything to avoid spending the afternoon with Marshal Barrett.

Her father gave her a frown and turned to the marshal. "Do you mind going along, Barrett? Samantha knows where all the good holes are."

The marshal gave her a long look, and Samantha held her breath, hoping he'd have some reason to decline. Failing health? Fear of water? Fear of fish?

"Ed, for home-cooked trout I'd be willing to do just about anything."

4

Samantha dug into her can of corn, baited her hook, and tossed her line into the fast-moving river. She'd just had the longest morning of her life.

She'd gone through the motions of doing her chores, but in the back of her mind lingered the idea that she would soon be meeting up with Marshal Barrett and they would be going down to the river to fish away the afternoon. She was terrified of being alone with him. And seeing him standing on the porch after lunch, dressed in a pair of tight buckskin pants and a creamy white shirt, hadn't helped her state of mind one bit.

"Why do you use corn?"

Startled, she glanced over to where he sat on the rocky bank. As he gazed at her the soft breeze lifted his hair from his eyes, and she wondered if she'd imagined their confrontation the night before. "It tastes better than worms."

He smiled. "You know that for a fact?"

"What would you think if I said yes?"

"I'd think you put an awful lot of effort into fishing."

She looked back at her line to hide her smile. "The fish bite better with corn."

"I see. . . . And do they bite better when you're wearing pants?"

She glanced down at her brown trousers. "I wouldn't know. I've never fished in a dress."

"Today would've been a good day to start."

Now, that was an odd thing to say. She looked over at him, but he'd turned his attention back to his line. "Do you have a problem with women wearing pants, Mr. Barrett?"

"As long as they don't fit better than mine."

Samantha glanced over at his tight buckskins and wondered why they hadn't split down the seam by now. "Those would be hard to beat."

"What?"

"I said, why don't *you* try fishing in a dress sometime and see how comfortable it is?"

"I think I'll take your word for it."

Samantha broke into a full blown smile, picturing him in her green muslin with the wide flounce.

"I smell something sweet."

She eased her line a little closer to the shore. "It's the apple trees. They're in full bloom this time of year."

"It's beautiful here. Must be difficult for you to leave."

The breeze picked up, and pine needles drifted down around them from the trees overhead. "Yes, Mr. Barrett, it is."

"Nobody's forcing you to do it, Miss James."

"No, but I've obligated myself, and I am looking forward to starting a life of my own."

He laughed softly and shook his head.

"You find that funny?"

"No. Some people just don't appreciate what they have until they lose it, that's all. Once you leave, you can never really come back home, you know?"

"Are you trying to tell me not to go to Utah?"

He grew serious. "Would you consider staying?"

She narrowed her eyes. "Why is it I'm starting to get the impression that you're determined to *make* me consider it?"

"You have a nibble, Miss James."

"What?"

"I said, you have a nibble!" He jumped up.

Samantha gasped as her pole was yanked from her hands. She didn't just have a nibble, she had a full-fledged bite.

The marshal dove for her pole, which was quickly floating downriver, and landed on it, face first in the water. Samantha covered her eyes, and when she finally did look it was to see Marshal Barrett striding to shore, water pouring off his plastered cotton shirt and tight buckskins. He held up her pole. "The fish got away."

She felt her lips twitch, and she tried to hold back, but in the end she let out a loud burst of laughter. "You . . . you didn't have to do that."

He wiped the water off his face. "I thought I should at least save your pole."

"But I have three more of them at home."

He scowled. "You could have kept that little piece of information to yourself."

She covered her mouth with her hand to keep herself from laughing any more, but it didn't work. "That water looks very cold."

He arched a brow. "Why not try it yourself?" He ran his fingers through his hair and flicked the water into her face.

Samantha sputtered but went right on laughing. So the marshal crouched down, scooped up a handful of river and tossed it on her.

Samantha screeched—it was, indeed, very cold. She bent down and started splashing him back. Before they were finished, they were both soaked to the skin, and they'd scared away any fish they might have caught.

She was knee-deep in the cold river and out of breath. He was wringing the water out of his shirt tails when she started laughing again. "Dad's going to be upset that you won't get trout for dinner."

"I may not get to eat the fish, Miss James but,"— he wiped the river water from his lips—"I've tasted them just the same."

She turned for the bank, but when her right foot landed on a mossy rock it flew out from under her. The whole world went sideways, and she almost landed back in the water, but the marshal caught her and helped her to the shore. His strong hands were on her hips, and she felt his heat clear through her cold, wet clothes.

"These pants have got to be two sizes too small," he said from behind her.

"I could say the same for yours." She turned toward him only to be confronted with an expression she couldn't have mistaken.

Desire.

Dear God, he was attracted to her, just as she was attracted to him.

He was staring at her mouth. "Do we stop pretending now?" he asked, tightening his hands around her back.

"I don't know what you mean." She saw the burning in his eyes, realized he was going to kiss her, and stepped back from him so fast she almost stumbled again.

He set his hands on his waist and watched her intently.

"We should be getting back," she said finally.

The flame had faded from his eyes. "Yeah, I suppose we should be."

She didn't wait to be sure he was following but set off down the trail at a brisk pace, telling herself she'd handled the situation well—even though her body was still burning where he'd touched it.

* * *

"What do you mean you didn't catch anything? The two of you have been gone close to three hours. . . . Looks like you had time for a swim."

Samantha clenched her hands in front of her, refusing to look at Marshal Barrett. "A fish took my pole Daddy, and the marshal tried to save it. He fell in the river."

"A fish took your pole? What, did the thing sneak up on the bank when you weren't looking and snatch it out of your hands?"

"It was a big fish, Ed. The damn thing yanked the pole right out of her hands."

"And you tried to save the pole? She's got three more of them in the barn."

"Yeah, I know."

"And what about you?" he said to Samantha. "How the devil did you get so wet?"

"I—well, we—"

"Samantha slipped on a rock and fell in."

"Samantha fell in? Well, are you O.K., honey? I thought you knew enough to watch out for those slippery rocks."

She did, when she wasn't distracted by a tall, golden god with hands like fire. "Daddy, the fish aren't that important. I'll just fix us up some scones and preserves. I'll slice some ham and warm it— we'll have a real nice supper."

"Scones and ham—I wanted to feed the boy trout, Sam!"

"Remember, Daddy, the marshal doesn't like it when you call him 'Boy.'" She smiled, patted her father's hand, and hurried off to her room to change and collect herself before her father could say anything more.

She stripped off her wet shirt and pants, all the while chanting to herself that she wasn't going to get involved. So what if the marshal had experienced a quick flash of desire? The man wandered the countryside for months at a time and probably rarely found himself alone with a woman—which didn't leave her much hope on their two-week trip, now that she thought about it.

She covered her face with her hands. Things were going from bad to worse. Before, when she'd been the only one afflicted by this attraction, she'd only had to worry about herself. But now she would have to worry about the marshal jumping out at her from behind some bush on the trail and fulfilling the promise that had been in his eyes a half hour ago.

5

Samantha stood at the kitchen window, watching the sun rise on her last day in Spokane Falls. Golden rays of sunshine lifted over the mountainous horizon and began to dry up the morning dew.

She poured two steaming cups of coffee. The marshal wasn't up yet, and she was glad, because she was going to need some time to talk her father out of the ridiculous idea he'd come up with that morning.

She set his cup of coffee in front of him at the table. "Daddy, if I wanted Marshal Barrett to take me to the party, I'd ask him myself."

"I'd just feel so much better if he were there, Sam, just in case that Duncan fella tries somethin'."

"Daddy, what do you think Randy might do? Snatch

me from the party and drag me off by my hair? He's not any more interested in me than I am in him."

"I was talking to Amos at the mercantile just Wednesday and he told me Randy was jawing all over town about how he planned to win you back at this little shindig."

"That's ridiculous. Amos is always spouting off at the mouth. Remember when he told you Mary Beth Baxter was the cousin of the Queen of England? And all because she wore that stupid tiara to the winter carnival."

"Just the same, Sam, I'd feel a whole lot better if you had an escort."

Samantha dropped her head into her hands and sighed.

"Had an escort to what?"

She looked up to see Marshal Barrett standing in the doorway and felt herself flush. "Nothing, Marshal. Have a seat and I'll get you some breakfast."

"Uh, is it eggs again?"

She glared at him, wanting more than ever to wipe the smile from his face. "No, Mr. Barrett, it's biscuits and gravy."

As she fixed him a plate she silently begged her father to see reason and not ask the marshal to be her escort, but to no avail.

"There's a favor I'd like you to do for me, Barrett."

She prayed the floor would swallow her up.

"There's this barn dance tonight, a going-away party for Sam, actually, and I don't like the idea of her attending it alone, considering Randy'll probably be there and all."

"And you'd like for me to take her."

The marshal looked her way, and Samantha felt her heart drop down into her stomach. She'd had very disturbing dreams the night before about Max Barrett. She could feel her ears begin to turn pink just at the memory.

"Really, it's not necessary, Mr. Barrett. My father is overreacting. I'll be fine on my own."

The marshal shrugged. "I wouldn't mind going."

"But I thought you'd be spending the evening making preparations for our trip."

"We'll *both* be making preparations for our trip *today*, Miss James. We'll need to ride into town with a wagon to stock up on supplies."

"We? *We* will be riding into town?"

"Sam, the man's your escort, not your slave. You can't expect him to do everything. And don't you worry about that party. Barrett doesn't mind going one bit."

The marshal grinned at her, and she felt a spark of irritation. Those eyes of his put the whole darn sky to shame.

One look from those eyes and a woman would jump to do his bidding.

Samantha grit her teeth. She had a feeling the next time she saw Melissa Cauldwell she was going to sock her straight in the nose.

* * *

The wagon jangled toward town, and Samantha's nerves jangled right along with it. Yesterday morning she'd wanted the trip to Utah put on hold indefinitely, but now she couldn't wait to get on the trail, to get the whole thing over with so she could get this unsettling man out of her life.

The marshal sat next to her on the buckboard with the reins in his hands. She hadn't seen him since breakfast that morning, but that hadn't stopped her thoughts of him from interrupting her chores and distracting her at all the wrong moments. She'd slopped the pigs with the morning milk and put the chicken feed in the ice house.

"Does your leg always jitter like that?"

She looked down. Her leg was bouncing around like a Mexican jumping bean. She clamped one of her hands down on her knee and redirected her gaze to the road.

"I make you nervous, don't I?"

He was so arrogant it made her teeth grind.

"It's perfectly O.K., Miss James. As a matter of fact, it happens all the time."

Arrogant, arrogant, arrogant.

"Six foot five inches of a man tends to make a woman a little skittish."

They rolled into town and down Main Street, stopping in front of Amos's mercantile. The marshal helped her down from the wagon. "Kind of romantic, isn't it?"

She gave him an odd look.

He motioned to the boardwalk beneath his feet. "This is where we met for the very first time."

She rolled her eyes. "A moment I'll never forget."

He placed his hand in the small of her back and led her into the mercantile. "And now we're on our first shopping trip. Sort of brings tears to your eyes, doesn't it?"

"I will get the canned goods, Mr. Barrett. Why don't you take yourself over to the other side of the store and look at the dog muzzles?"

Then she realized that the mercantile had fallen quiet. She looked into the surprised faces of Amos Clemens, and two ladies she knew who were also apparently shopping. And then she saw the reason for their silent stares: Randy was standing at the counter buying his weekly supply of cigarette fixings.

She hesitated for a moment and then lifted her chin and went about her business. She refused to let Randy Duncan have any more impact on her life than he already had.

She set her mind on counting out ten cans each of carrots, corn, and peas, and twenty cans of beans. She heard the familiar thump of Randy's boots as he approached behind her.

"Sam?"

She told herself she would not turn around. But he didn't move away. Finally she gave in. "What!"

Randy blinked in surprise. "Sam, I—I heard you were leavin' town."

"You heard right."

"I—I sure wish you wouldn't go."

She glanced over at the marshal, who was on the other side of the room looking at horse blankets. She wondered if he knew her ex-fiancé was in the store. "Why?"

"Huh?"

"Why don't you want me to go?"

"Well, gee, Sam. You know why. This whole thing . . . this whole thing has all been an awful misunderstandin'."

"And what, exactly, is it about this *thing* that you feel I've misunderstood?"

"Me and Julia," he said under his breath. "This whole thing between me and Julia. We were . . . we were just dancin'."

Samantha caught herself before she laughed out loud. She looked over Randy's shoulder at the two ladies straining to hear every word they were saying. "What I saw in my barn three weeks ago was not a reel or even a waltz. It looked more like an odd form of leapfrog."

"Shhh!"

"Oh, I'm sorry Mr. Duncan. Were you under the impression that this was all still a secret?"

Randy glanced back and smiled faintly at their audience before turning back to Samantha. "You're only damagin' your reputation by making this town business."

"What's the matter, Mr. Duncan? Did your new

sweetheart catch you in the orchards with Yolanda Fields?"

The look on Randy's face was worth every bit of gossip she'd had to listen to in order to get this vital piece of information.

"Why, you vindictive little witch! You can't stand the idea of me leavin' you at the altar and now you're tryin' to tarnish the reputations of two very upstandin' young ladies."

"Oh, I doubt they're upstanding when you're around, Mr. Duncan. As a matter of fact, I'm sure they're *downlying* in the tall grass."

Randy's face turned red, and Samantha heard an odd sound come from Marshal Barrett, who still appeared fascinated by those horse blankets. "You've turned into a harpy, and don't think I don't know the reason! It's that marshal, ain't it?"

Samantha didn't say a word. She just stood there and stared at Randy, wondering when he'd lost his mind or if he'd ever really had one.

"He gotcha, didn't he? He got his pig into your poke!"

She felt her cheeks flame, and she reached behind her to grab a hefty can of food. She saw the marshal coming toward Randy, but it was too late to stop the forward motion of her arm. She threw the can . . . and missed. Well, she sort of missed. Instead of hitting Randy, she got Marshal Barrett square between the eyes.

The marshal stumbled back and sent produce

display tumbling, scattering apples across the floor. While he tried to gain his feet amidst all the rolling fruit, Randy darted out of the mercantile.

Samantha didn't know what to do. She could only stand there with her eyes wide and her hands covering her mouth. "I'm sorry," she whispered. "I'm so sorry."

Amos Clemens helped the marshal to his feet. "That's some arm ya got there, Miss James," Amos said, grinning.

Marshal Barrett, his hand pressed between his eyes, regained his feet and glanced toward the door where Randy had made his escape.

"I'm sorry," Samantha said again.

"She was trying to nail that Duncan feller."

The marshal nodded. "I don't suppose you have any ice in the back?"

Amos skittered off to the back of the store just as the two other customers snuck out the front door. "There they go," Samantha grumbled. "Those two will spread this mess across town before you can blink an eye."

"I'm having a little trouble doing that right now."

"Oh, Mr. Barrett, I'm really very sorry." She took his arm and sat him down on a barrel of flour. She pulled his hand off his face and grimaced at red mark between his eyebrows. "You have to know I didn't mean to hit you. Actually, I'm surprised I hit a thing."

Amos came forward with a chunk of ice and a

towel. Samantha wrapped the ice and pressed it carefully against the marshal's wound. "Are . . . are you okay? Do you feel dizzy? Maybe we should get the doctor."

"Just give me a second, Miss James. It's not everyday a man is blindsided by a can of peas."

She flinched at his harsh tone. "I told you I'm very sorry."

"Yes, you've said that a number of times."

"I—I'll just get back to the cans and have Amos load what we need into the wagon."

"Hell, girl, why don't ya just toss 'em in from here."

Samantha didn't appreciate Amos's remark, or his broad smile. With his imagination, she'd probably be pitching for the Cincinnati Red Stockings by suppertime.

6

Samantha sat on the buckboard, wearing her best lilac dress, waiting for Marshal Barrett. The party had started well over an hour ago, but the marshal had just woken up from a very long afternoon nap.

She'd checked up on him a few times just to be sure he was still alive. One never knew when it came to a blow to the head. He seemed to be all right, but that can of peas had apparently knocked the get-up-and-go right out of him and had left a faint green bruise between his sky-blue eyes.

He finally came out of the house and climbed up onto the wagon. Samantha only had a second to admire him in his black pants and white cotton shirt before he snapped the reins and sent the wagon plunging forward.

She was jerked backward and gave him a glare.

"You know, I've apologized to you a number of times, Mr. Barrett. When are you going to stop being so angry with me?"

"I'm not angry with you, Miss James. Forgive me if I seem a little dazed. Your father has asked me to tell you not to let Randy Duncan talk you into anything stupid tonight."

His tone certainly sounded angry to her. "Talk me into what?"

"Your father feels that Duncan's going to try to get you back."

"Why would Randy do that? He's told the whole town that he left me high and dry—"

"Which will make him look all the more considerate when he agrees to give you a second chance."

This reasoning startled Samantha. "Do you really think he'll try something?"

He gave her a long look. "I would."

Samantha looked away. Surely she'd misunderstood him. He merely meant that if he loved a woman as much as Randy had professed to love her, then he would try to get that woman back.

"You don't have to worry, Marshal. I'm not about to forgive what I saw that day, or forget."

"Exactly what was it you saw that started this whole mess?"

She fiddled with the bow on her dress. Apparently, her father hadn't told him everything. "They were . . . Randy and Julia were . . . well . . . you know . . . in the barn."

His brows raised. "And you saw them . . . you knowing?"

"Plain as daylight."

"Interesting."

"If you're a dog breeder."

He laughed and turned the horses toward the row of wagons coming up on the side of the road. He stopped at the end of the parking line, climbed down, and held a hand out to Samantha.

They walked into the brightly lit barn and, after greeting the Parkers near the door, Sam introduced Marshal Barrett to Sheriff Brown and Mayor Philips. Then she came face to face with Flora Miller and gave the young woman a pasty smile. Flora's normally pale face was red, evidently flushed from a recent turn on the dance floor.

"So you decided to show up after all," Flora said. "We were all starting to think that Randy had broken your heart so badly you wouldn't make it to your own going-away party."

"Sorry to disappoint you, Flora. Have you met Marshal Barrett?"

Flora turned to Max Barrett and gave him a once over with her eyes. Samantha felt a moment of unbridled triumph. *That's right, Flora,* she thought. *I'm not heartbroken over Randy, I've simply traded him in for something better.*

The marshal took Flora's plump hand and greeted her politely while a plan began to spin in Samantha's head—a plan that would really give these people something to talk about on her last night in town.

Once the marshal was done greeting Flora, Samantha pushed her arm through his and edged up close to his side. He looked down at her in surprise, but Samantha saw Flora arch a brow, which told her she'd more than accomplished her purpose.

"Have you two known each other long?" Flora asked.

"Actually—" Marshal Barrett began.

"Long enough," Samantha cut in. "Max is staying with Dad and me."

Flora's eyes rounded, obviously recognizing a juicy piece of gossip when she heard one. "Oh, darn," she said. "There's Alice Hornsby. I really must go speak with her. Talk to you later, Samantha."

Samantha grinned as Flora dashed away, making a beeline to the circle of young women that included Julia Thorn. Then she glanced up at the marshal. The ice in his gaze froze the smile on her lips and made her take a step away from him.

"What are you doing?" he demanded.

Samantha laughed nervously. "Well . . . I just thought that since we're here together, we could be, well . . . here to—"

Max bent down and spoke distinctly into her face. "I am your escort, Miss James. Nothing more. You start giving these people something besides that to gnaw on and you'll be getting in way over your head."

He walked away, leaving her feeling about two inches tall, and struck up a conversation with some people across the room. Then she watched him begin a waltz with Reverend Parker's wife.

His legs moved gracefully in his black trousers, and his broad shoulders bunched beneath his white cotton shirt as he swayed. If she hadn't made him so angry it would be her dancing with him now.

She was standing alone on the sidelines when the gang of gossips fell upon her like a pack of feeding sharks.

"Don't tell me another one's left you," Flora said.

"Oh my, girls, look," Alice Hornsby said, snickering while pointing at Max on the dance floor. "The marshal's thrown Samantha over for the Reverend's old wife!"

A chorus of giggles followed, and Samantha glared at them as they flounced away. Thrown her over? She would show them!

Rising from her seat, she moved toward the dance floor, taking a quick swig of punch as she passed the refreshment table. She worked her way through the crowd of dancing people and tapped Irma Parker on the shoulder.

"I'd like to cut in," she said, avoiding the marshal's eyes.

Irma Parker looked a little bewildered. "All right, dear."

Samantha moved into the circle of Max's arms.

She chanced a peek at his face and saw that his eyes were glittering with anger.

"Irma Parker seems to think we're engaged," he said. "She wanted to congratulate me on my fine catch. You can imagine her embarrassment when I told her that we aren't really seeing each other at all, that this whole rumor is your childish revenge on a wandering man."

"You didn't tell her that!"

"No, but *you* will."

Samantha caught sight of Flora, Alice, and Julia Thorn watching them. "Could you hold me a little closer, please?"

He looked over at the circle of young women. "How 'bout if I strangle you instead?" Despite his gruff reply, he did heed her request.

Samantha's chest pressed against his, but she hardly noticed the contact. She was too busy wrapping her arm around his neck and looking out of the corner of her eye to make sure everyone that mattered was watching.

Max held his breath and moved still closer to Samantha, melding her body into his own. Her smooth, silken arm slipped further around his neck. Not able to help himself, he spanned her slim waist with his hand and dipped his head to her ear. He caught the faint flowery scent of apple blossoms as tendrils of her loosely bound hair tickled his nose.

At that moment his desire for her overcame all else, and he grazed his teeth over the sweet skin of her neck.

She squeezed his chin with her shoulder, and he was trapped for a moment before she pulled back. "What are you doing?" she asked.

"Living the part?"

"You're tickling me." She gave him a strange look. "Are you all right? You look a little flushed. I still think you should have seen the doctor."

His eyes roamed her perfect features, his breath coming fast as he stared at her soft, pale lips. Crazy as it sounded, at that moment he would have given anything for just one kiss.

And he almost took it.

Then Randy Duncan spun Samantha around by the arm. "I'm cuttin' in."

A pure territorial instinct narrowed Max's eyes, and he took a step toward the boy, intending to lay him out flat on the floor.

Samantha stepped in between them. "I have no intention of dancing with you, Randy Duncan." Heads turned in their direction. "Go dance with Julia Thorn!"

"What are you doin' all pressed up against this lawman!"

"None of your business!"

"Are you two really gettin' married?"

Max's mind was beginning to clear, now that Samantha was a few feet away from him. He remained silent, waiting to see how Samantha would handle the young man's question.

"Well, I—I don't know where you heard that from," she said. "We certainly haven't announced anything."

Max had to give her credit. That was a damn good sidestep.

"If you will excuse us now, Mr. Duncan, the marshal and I were enjoying a dance."

She turned back toward him, but Randy Duncan wasn't about to give up. Max figured the boy's courage had more to do with the spiked punch and the watching crowd than any desire he might still have for Samantha. Randy clamped a hand down on her shoulder and spun her back around.

Determined to take care of this whole matter calmly and reasonably, Max said, "Mr. Duncan, the young lady does not want to dance with you. I suggest you get yourself some air."

Randy looked up at him—one advantage of his height was that everybody had to look up at him. "Stay out of this, Marshal. You may have had your way with her, but she's still my fiancée."

Samantha gasped, and Max closed his eyes for a second. Calm and reasonable had just gone straight out the window. Now he was going to have the pleasure of punching Randy Duncan's lights out.

But before he could take care of business, he felt something hard catch him across the side of the head. He staggered and opened his eyes to see

Randy crouched down and Samantha looking stunned, holding a solid wooden cane.

The damn woman had whopped him again!

Samantha stood across the room from Max, watching as he talked to everybody in the room but her. He was mad at her again, and rightfully so, she supposed. But how could she have known that Randy was going to duck at just the right moment? How could she have known the walking stick would be so heavy she wouldn't be able to control her aim of it?

"Oh, Sam! Can you believe the man we met on the boardwalk was your marshal?"

Samantha gave Melissa a faint smirk. "It's about time you got here. And to think you ran me up the flagpole because I didn't want to come. That hat looks wonderful, by the way."

"Don't change the subject. I've only been here five minutes, and I've already heard rumors about the two of you. Are you engaged to that handsome thing?"

"No. It's just sort of spread into that."

"Well, in that case, introduce me."

Samantha gave Melissa a hard look. "Fine. Come on."

She walked straight through the crowd of women surrounding the marshal and interrupted his conversation with the schoolteacher. "Excuse me, Miss Staples. Max Barrett, meet my friend, Melissa Cauldwell."

He was still furious with her, Samantha could tell by the way he barely looked at her. For Melissa, however, he had a charming smile. "I was beginning to doubt Samantha had any friends."

"You seem to have acquired a few of your own, Marshal," Samantha replied, eyeing the woman standing next to him.

"Why, yes. Amanda and I have a lot in common."

"Amanda?" No one in the whole town had ever called the skinny teacher anything but Miss Staples.

Max smiled down at the woman, and Samantha's face heated with a bad case of jealousy. She suddenly couldn't stand the heat or the crowd. "I think I need some air," she said and hurried out of the barn.

Once outside, she took two big gulps of air and rubbed the goose flesh prickling her arms in the chill of the night. She laughed at herself, at the fool she was once again becoming over a man. Would she ever learn?

She heard the marshal call her name, heard the crunching of his boots as he approached, but she kept her back to him. She wasn't ready to face him yet.

"Are you ready to leave, Samantha?"

"I wouldn't want to take you away from anything, Mr. Barrett." She recognized the biting sound of jealousy in her voice and squeezed her eyes shut in disgust with herself.

The marshal's hands came down on her bare shoulders, and a tremor raced up her spine, one he had to have noticed. He rested his chin on the top of her head. "It's a beautiful night."

She looked up at the stars, and her eyes filled with tears.

"See the North Star?"

She shook her head, not able to see a thing but a blurry black sky.

He put his face next to hers and lifted her chin in the right direction. "See it?" he said close to her ear.

She blinked her eyes clear. "Yes."

"That'll be our compass in the mountains."

She sniffed. "And on the nights when it's cloudy?"

"Those will be the nights when you'll have to trust me."

"I—I'm sorry I hit you with the stick."

"I know you are."

She turned toward him. "No. I really am very sorry."

She made the mistake of looking up into his eyes, and then she was lost, trapped in a warm, inviting sea of blue.

"I'm sorry too, Samantha."

It was as if in a dream, the way he bent his head and captured her lips. Stunned at first, Samantha stiffened and tried to back away, but he tucked his hands into her hair and kept her close.

He had a sensuous, lazy way of kissing that drove her senses wild and she had to brace her hands against his chest to stay upright. She didn't want this. She'd told herself that a hundred times. But, want it or not, she was coming alive beneath Max Barrett's tender assault.

7

Max hurried after Samantha as she rushed from the wagon and into the house. The screen door bounced off the outside wall with a loud crash, and Ed James looked up from his paper. Samantha was breathing as if she'd run all the way home.

Ed stood up. "What'd he do now, Sam?"

"He kissed me, that's what he did!"

Ed seemed to relax, and Max thought that maybe he wouldn't be chased with a shotgun that night after all.

"Well, did you give the rascal a good sock in the nose?"

Samantha glared at Max. "I didn't think of it at the time."

Ed turned his attention to Max. "He didn't do anything but kiss her, right?"

At that point it dawned on Max that Ed and Samantha weren't talking about the same man. "Ed, I think you're a little confus—"

"What were you doing during all this?"

"He was mauling me against the wagon, that's what he was doing!"

Now Ed really looked confused. "Randy mauled you against the wagon?"

"What the hell does Randy have to do with any of this!" Samantha shouted.

"Well, plenty, I would think!"

"Daddy, it was your precious Mr. Barrett! He's the one who kissed me!" And with that, she stomped off to her room and slammed the door.

Max figured he could count the minutes he was going to live on one hand, but then he noticed that Ed James looked more startled than mad. "*You* kissed Samantha?"

"Unfortunately, yes."

"You must kiss like a son-of-a-bitch, my friend. She's madder than a wet cat left out in a blizzard."

"I did apologize to her."

Ed raised his brows. "Did you?"

"Before I kissed her."

"Before?"

"In case I forgot to afterwards."

Ed paced back and forth. "This certainly puts a kink in things, doesn't it? I think you and I are going to need to set some ground rules."

"Such as?"

"Samantha may not look it, Barrett, but she's still hurt by what Duncan did. Understandable or not, she was ready to spend the rest of her life with that boy, and he destroyed every ounce of trust she had in him. And that wasn't the first time. Two years ago a rotten local boy twisted her heart around his little finger and then stomped on it the same way. I want your word of honor that you won't take advantage of my daughter on the trail."

"Take advan—"

"Your word of honor."

"Dammit! If you don't trust me, why in the hell do you still want me to squire her through the mountains?"

"You give me your word and I'll trust you. We'll leave it at that."

Max considered his options. If he refused, chances were he'd be let off the hook and he could get himself and his raging urges away from Samantha James. But he'd said he'd do the task, and dammit, after having seen two run-ins with Randy Duncan, he could understand Samantha's reasons for wanting to leave.

"All right. You've got my word. But, Christ, Ed, it was just one lousy kiss."

"Uh huh, and I aim to make sure you won't be practicing to make it any better. What time you planning on leavin' tomorrow?"

"Before noon."

"Then we'll see ya in the morning."

Max headed down the hall to his room.

"She's not gonna forgive you for this too soon, ya know," Ed called after him. Max could have sworn he heard laughter in the man's voice. "Better watch your back for the next few days."

Max glanced at Samantha's door. "I guess sometimes children hold grudges."

Samantha tore furiously at the buttons on her clothes. She pulled the dress over her head and threw it on the floor, where it fell in a mass of lilac folds.

She kicked off her black shoes and pulled her legs out of her bloomers, which also ended up in a heap. Then she removed a warm flannel nightgown from her bureau and tossed it over her head. If Max Barrett ever tried to kiss her again, she'd tear his lips clean off his face!

She slipped under the covers of her bed and turned down the lamp.

It wasn't that she hadn't enjoyed the kiss. The truth was, she'd liked it a whole lot. It was just that he'd had no right to do it! He wasn't courting her, and he certainly hadn't asked her permission. He wasn't even repentant now. He'd actually had the audacity to apologize *before* he'd done it!

He was arrogant and smug. And immoral. He'd put his tongue in her mouth!

She rolled over and burrowed her head into her

pillow. She'd heard what Max had just said outside her door. Well, if he thought she was such a child, then why had he had his hands all over her not thirty minutes ago?

He was a pompous old fool! He had to be forty years old—well, at least thirty. She loved the way his eyes crinkled when he smiled, but not so much that she'd let him get away with unwelcome advances. Well, maybe not unwelcome, but unexpected just the same!

His moustache was soft, as she'd hoped it would be. She would have thought a thick moustache like that would be prickly, but it was smooth and silky, like the hair she'd felt at the back of his neck. And his big hands had been strong and warm as they'd roamed over her back. All in all, she supposed it had been a rather nice kiss. Not fumbling and aggressive like Randy's, but smooth, practiced, enveloping.

She squeezed her eyes shut in the darkness and tried to force the experience from her memory, but the feel of his mouth on hers lingered.

She was in trouble. Deep trouble.

The rooster crowed, and Max sat straight up in his bed. It was morning already, and he'd barely gotten any sleep.

Rubbing his hands briskly over his face, he glanced down at the blanket covering his legs. His arousal was obvious. "It was only one lousy kiss," he said aloud.

But that one lousy kiss had kept him up most of the night with fantasies about what it would be like to have more. Last night he'd been insulted that Ed had extracted a promise from him, but this morning he was relieved.

He stretched his arms and yawned. A good hearty breakfast was what he needed. Then he would set things straight with Samantha, tell her he'd gotten lost in the moment or something, and they would be on their way. He dressed quickly and walked down the hall to the kitchen.

Squinting his eyes in the bright sunlight coming in through the window, he made out the odd sight of Ed cooking at the stove. He looked around, finding himself surprisingly relieved that Samantha was nowhere to be seen. "Where's the sprite?"

Ed turned to him. His face was splotched with flour, and grease stains ran all down the front of his shirt and trousers. "How should I know? She's punishing you, and I'm caught up in the middle. I imagine she rode off before we even got up this morning, and most likely won't be back until we've poisoned each other." He threw a sticky glob of biscuit dough onto the counter, where it stuck, probably never to be removed again.

Max rubbed the back of his neck. He'd have no hearty breakfast today, but he supposed he deserved no better.

Ed tossed a spoon into the sink, and it clattered loudly on the dishes Samantha hadn't done. "He kisses her and I'm penalized," he grumbled. "Maybe if I'd a'shot him I'd a'gotten a decent breakfast."

"I'll go talk to her—"

"Just leave the girl alone. Sit your butt down and I'll try to make somethin' that won't come back up."

It was two hours past sunrise, and Samantha knew the men would have eaten by now, or if not they'd be sitting at the table, hungry, waiting for her. Either way, their stomachs would be in upheaval. Giving her brown speckled mare a kick, she rode off in the direction of the house.

When she reached the yard she found the marshal sitting alone on the front stoop. The moustache that had tickled her nose the night before was bent up on one side in a crooked smile.

"'Morning, Samantha."

"'Morning, Marshal," she replied, climbing down from her horse with her nose in the air.

"Where you been?"

"I had a few friends to visit."

He broke into a deep chuckle. "You are a vengeful woman. That breakfast your father made oughta take about a month to go all the way through me."

"Maybe next time you'll keep your lips to yourself."

"You wanted that kiss as badly as I did."

"Don't fool yourself." She climbed the porch steps and tried to walk past him, but he reached out and took ahold of her ankle.

"Your father got a promise out of me last night."

She couldn't find the courage to look down at him. "A promise?"

"A promise that I wouldn't take advantage of you on the trail."

"And do you always do what you're told?"

"Most of the time."

"What if I told you to never kiss me again?"

He hesitated. "You don't want that any more than I do."

She looked away from his magnetic blue gaze. "Sometimes what we want isn't always what's best for us. I suggest you hold to your promise."

He stretched his legs and stood. "I plan to. Now, everything's all packed up. We'll leave as soon as you're ready."

Samantha glanced through the front door and saw her father sitting in his chair by the fireplace. Would she ever really be ready? Tears clogged her throat. It was time to leave. It was time to say good-bye.

She looked back at the marshal. "Could you . . . ?"

"I'll get your bedroll on your horse and meet you out front when you're ready."

She pushed open the screen and went into the house. Her father looked up at her with moisture in his eyes. "'Bout time to go?"

"Yeah."

She took his hand. "I'm going to"—her voice broke—"I'm going to miss you."

He stood from the chair and pulled her into his arms. She pressed her face against his familiar, broad chest and forced herself not to cry.

"I'm proud of you, Sam. You're makin' the right decision."

She looked up at him and smiled. Somehow his respect made everything a whole lot easier.

He kissed her hard on the forehead and turned her toward the door. "Now, you see that poor fella out there in the gray hat?"

Samantha stared out at the marshal, who was waiting on his horse.

"Go easy on him, Sam. And trust him. He'll get ya there safe."

He propelled her through the door and to her horse. As she climbed into the saddle, Marshal Barrett shook hands with her father, and they exchanged a few words she wasn't close enough to hear. Then the marshal kicked his horse in the direction of the mountains in the distance. Samantha started forward, and the pack mule followed close behind.

She glanced back one last time at her father, who stood on the porch waving. A rush of tears flooded her vision. The die had been cast. She would follow her head instead of her heart, for a change, and hope that everything would work out for the better.

8

Samantha slipped down from her mare after a long day of riding. She was sore from head to toe. While her horse drank from the nearby stream, she soaked a cloth in the cold water and used it to wipe her face, neck, and arms. Night was falling. They'd been riding for over ten hours.

She looked up and watched Marshal Barrett dip his hat into the water and pour it over his head. "Hungry?" he asked.

"Enough to eat your horse."

His smile was faint and fleeting. "I'll build a fire."

She watched him begin to clear an area, wondering if she would get any more conversation out of him than she had the entire day. They hadn't spoken three words to each other. She pictured her father sitting beside the fire at home reading his newspaper and knew that, tonight of all nights, she needed some companionship.

She straightened up and went to the pack mule for some pans and food. "How do peas and . . . sugared beans sound?"

"You mean for dinner or as projectiles?"

She glared at him, but he was too busy snapping dry branches for the fire to notice. She unloaded what she would need for dinner and then set to work laying her bedroll on the ground by the fire circle. The marshal cleared his throat loudly, and she turned to find him observing her.

"Miss James? You may want to clear the ground before you lay out that bedroll or you're going to be sleeping with some pretty unaccommodating rocks in your back. And at that range, one spark and you're gonna *be* the fire."

She lifted a corner of her bedroll and looked beneath. Barrett was right. There were small rocks everywhere. She moved a few feet away from the fire circle and got down on her hands and knees to toss the stones aside.

"You best put that bottom of yours somewhere besides in my face or I'm gonna use it as a table."

She looked over her shoulder at him and sat back on her feet. He was crouched by the fire, feeding the flames. "If my position is bothering you, Mr. Barrett, why don't you simply avert your eyes?"

He laughed. "That's like asking a man who just struck gold to leave it where it is."

Irritated, she pointed her *bottom* in the other direction and continued with her task. "Daddy says you live in Carson City."

"My family lives in Carson. I live wherever camp is for the night."

Samantha pried up a particularly nasty-looking rock and threw it into the stream. "Did you grow up in Carson?"

"I grew up in Boston."

She glanced up at him in surprise. He was Wild West from the toes of his cracked leather boots to the top of his gray western hat.

"Ten years of hard riding changes a man," he said as if in explanation.

"So you don't have a permanent home?"

"Carson. I just don't spend a lot of time there."

A barn owl hooted softly as the marshal continued to snap pieces of wood into kindling.

"Do you ever miss them, Mr. Barrett? Your family, I mean?"

"At first I missed them. Then your life sort of takes over and you only feel the loneliness every now and then, when you pause to think about it."

It was coming again, that same feeling that burned her eyes and tightened her throat. "Then I suppose I better keep my mind on something else," she said hoarsely.

There was a long pause, and then the marshal said, "Having second thoughts, Miss James? I warned you to get any misgivings out of your head before we left. Maybe you should have listened." He stood up and went to retrieve his bedroll.

"Loneliness does not warrant second thoughts. My decision to leave was the right one." She spread her blankets back over the ground she'd now cleared of rocks.

He dropped his bedroll and kneeled down beside her, flashing her a smile. "How can you be lonely when you've got me?"

"That's not such a difficult thing to accomplish."

"Ah, admit it, Miss James. I make you burn like a lit match."

"I beg your pardon?"

He spread out his bedroll, not bothering to clear his area at all, then he sat down and began opening their cans of food. "You sure you want beans our first night out?"

"Don't change the subject, Mr. Barrett. I want an explanation for what you just said."

"Well, beans tend to make a person—"

"Not an explanation about the beans, sir. An explanation for this burning *malhooey*. I hate to break this to you, but not only am I not attracted to you, I don't think I even *like* you."

The blasted man was grinning at her! He wasn't supposed to be grinning, he was supposed to be put down, set back in his place, hurt, for crying out loud!

He laughed, and she felt the distinct urge to strike him. "I'm sorry," he said, controlling himself.

"It's just that your eyes waver so badly when you lie—"

"I am not lying!"

He dumped the peas and the beans into separate pans and set them on the fire. "Let's not fight, Miss James. Not on our first night together."

"You started it! And don't think you're going to sleep that close to me."

He turned to her with a serious look for once. "There could be anything lurking in these mountains, and I'll sleep on top of you if that's what it takes to keep you safe."

She paled, not at the image of what horrible things lurked in the wilderness around her, but at the thought of Marshal Barrett sleeping on top of her. "I—I can protect myself."

"If that were the case you'd be making this trip by yourself, now, wouldn't you?"

She clamped her mouth shut and stared at the fire. It was impossible to win an argument with a mule, and that's exactly what Marshal Barrett was: a long-eared, twitchy-tailed, snorting, honking ass!

He woke her before the sun had completely risen and dropped a pistol on her stomach. "I'm going to look for some meat for breakfast. You stay put."

Samantha peered up at the brightening sky, and

looked around her at the thick forest, trying to orient herself. She'd slept terribly, rocks or not.

She sat up to watch the marshal disappear into the woods and then lifted the pistol. It fit neatly, even if a bit heavily, in the palm of her hand. She'd never fired anything but a shotgun before, but she assumed the technique would be the same.

She rose, packed up her bedroll, sponged herself off with water from the stream, and sat down to wait for the marshal's return.

The sun climbed in the sky. The sounds of nature surrounded her, growing louder as the day warmed. She tried to distract herself by drawing figures in the dirt with a stick, but all her energy was directed toward listening intently to every tiny noise.

Birds chirped, bees droned. If she listened carefully enough she could even hear the occasional *plunk* of a pinecone as it dropped from a tree.

A crow cawed loudly, and she jumped. Then she stood up and paced the tiny clearing, trying to calm herself. But the marshal had been gone for over two hours, and she was beginning to doubt that he planned to return. She hadn't exactly been nice to him the night before.

Her stomach growled.

A twig snapped nearby, and her heart nearly stopped. Then another sharp crack came from within the dense trees. Someone or something was coming. What if it wasn't the marshal?

Moving faster than her common sense would

allow, she grabbed the pistol and darted behind a large rock.

As the sounds grew louder, she called out, "Who's there?"

To her horror, nobody answered. She brought her hand in front of her and steadied the gun. As whoever it was pushed through the underbrush, she stood and fired, the shot ringing out across the mountainside.

9

"Shit!"

Max walked into the clearing, cursing a blue streak. Samantha gaped in surprise. She looked down at the smoking gun in her hand. "I thought you were—"

"What? A bear carrying a rabbit in one hand and a rifle in the other!"

"You should have answered me when I called out! How was I supposed to know who it was sneaking up on me?"

He snatched the gun from her hand. "I didn't answer you because I had another rabbit in my sights, Miss James. And never, *never* shoot at something until you know what the hell it is you're aiming at!"

She lifted her chin. She hated his ability to make

her feel like a naughty child. When she saw the skinned rabbit in his hand she grimaced. "I see your hunt was successful."

"I was hoping for two."

"I'm sorry! Do you always have to blame everything on me?"

"Forgive me, Miss James. I suppose I have no right to be upset with you when you've almost killed me three times in the past three days. Why don't you just get it over with and push me off a damn cliff?"

"Don't tempt me, Mr. Barrett."

He gave her a cold smile. "It's too late for that, Miss James, but I expect you to control yourself the same as I've sworn to do."

She clenched her fists and grit her teeth. One of these days she was going to win. One of these days she was going to argue him into the dust. She had two long weeks to give it her best try.

He moved toward the fire to prepare the rabbit for roasting over the flames. She went to her saddlebags and took out a bar of soap and a towel.

"I'm going further downstream to bathe—"

"No."

"No? You may be my guide, Mr. Barrett, but you are certainly not my father or my keeper. I will come and go as I see fit."

He looked up at her from across the fire, and she could see the reflection of the flames dancing in his bright eyes. "I suggest you stay close."

"Your suggestion is noted."

She walked downstream, thinking she just might be getting the hang of this verbal sparring. Her search for deeper water ended when she found a clear pool about waist deep. She quickly stripped off her pants and shirt and went into the water wearing only her camisole and pantelts. The water felt wonderful once she got used to the chill. She washed her body and her hair and then stretched out to float in the sunshine, eyes closed.

A shadow fell over her face, and she opened her eyes, expecting to find the marshal. But what she saw was much worse than any aggravating lawman: It was an Indian, tall, dark, and fierce looking. He was standing not five feet away from her, staring at her with intense brown eyes.

He reached out to touch her, and she screamed. The sound pierced the air and echoed off the mountains.

Then he said something in a language Samantha didn't understand, and she backed further into the stream, toward the opposite bank, wishing that she'd listened for once and stayed closer to camp.

"He says you're a goddess." Startled, Samantha looked over to where the marshal stood on the bank. "He says his people would honor him if he took you back to his camp."

The marshal spoke to the Indian in the Indian's language, and the tall, dark-haired man nodded and responded.

Samantha crossed her arms over her wet, practically transparent undergarments. Chills were beginning to wrack her body, whether from cold or fear she wasn't quite sure. "What's—what's he saying?"

"He wants you to be his third wife."

"No! Tell him not on his life!"

"Watch your tone. Whether you agree or not, he's offering you a great honor, Miss James. He certainly didn't have to ask permission. He could have scooped you up and carried you off."

"Don't you dare give—give me to him, Mr. Barrett! You're supposed to—to—"

"I have no intention of giving you to him, though the idea is tempting. Maybe it would teach you a lesson. If you'd stayed close to camp like I told you, none of this would be happening.

The Indian was still staring at her, and Samantha felt absolutely bare, naked to the world. "Can't you make him go away?" she whispered .

The marshal moved toward the savage with his hands open at his sides. He spoke to the Indian for what seemed like a long time, and finally the Indian turned and left.

Samantha was astounded. The savage had simply turned around without a backward glance and left them—alive and unharmed! She hurried out of the stream, protecting herself from the marshal's eyes as best she could, and wrapped herself up in the towel she'd brought with her.

"What did you say to make him leave?"

"I told him you were my wife."

She blinked. "And he gave up? Just like that?"

"No. He offered me two squaws, three mustangs, and four rifles for you."

"Thank goodness he accepted your refusal."

"I didn't refuse him."

"What do you mean, you didn't refuse him?"

"I told him I wanted two squaws, six mustangs, and ten rifles. He said no woman was worth that much, and left."

Samantha stared at him. "And what if he'd accepted your offer?"

The marshal laughed. "Then I would've had plenty of horses to pack home my squaws and rifles."

Max and Samantha mounted up by late morning and, with the sun beaming down on them through the thick trees, began their second day's ride. They wouldn't be stopping for lunch, so Max had divided up the rabbit to eat as they rode.

He was doing his best to ignore her. After being shot at and having his orders disobeyed he wasn't in the mood to play it nice with Miss Storm. She was lucky that Indian had been friendly, otherwise she might have found herself sporting braids and moccasins by now.

He could tell she was growing bored by the way

she kept fidgeting. Any second now she was bound to try and start talking again—

"Why did you become a marshal?"

He raised his head at the sound of her voice and glanced over at her. "Why do you want to know?"

"Just making conversation."

He smirked. Women were so predictable. "I wanted to see the country."

"That's hardly a reason to risk your life every day, Mr. Barrett."

"Maybe I'm the kind of man who thinks he can make a difference in the world."

"That's very noble. Now tell me the real reason."

"I could ride well, shoot straight, fight like a son-of-a-bitch, and the money was fair."

"And the danger never bothers you?"

"Just living is dangerous, lady."

They rode on for a while, and he watched a squirrel follow alongside them, dancing on narrow branches from tree to tree.

Samantha cleared her throat. "How many times have you been shot?"

He gave her a dubious look, thinking that with conversation like this she must be *desperate* for entertainment. "More than I've kept track of."

"And you've never wanted to quit?"

"Nope."

The squirrel seemed to have given up trying to chase them and darted deeper into the woods.

Max craned his neck and watched until he'd lost sight of it.

"How does your family feel about your profession?"

"They deal with it."

"They must worry about you when you're gone—which is apparently most of the time."

"Miss James, whether my family agrees or disagrees with my chosen occupation is, frankly, none of your damn business."

He kicked his horse and rode further ahead of her, hoping she'd take the hint. Not surprisingly, she didn't.

Soon her horse was edging up next to his again. "I can imagine they must hate what you do for a living."

"I'm a big boy. They don't have any say in what I do anymore. Now, I don't suppose you can imagine moving this conversation in another direction?"

She smiled, and he had to look away to keep from smiling back. "How about the weather?"

"Too obvious."

"Fashion?"

"The reemergence of the bustle is far from my favorite topic. How 'bout politics?"

She wrinkled her nose. "Too stuffy."

"About the only subject left is sheep herding, Miss James, and I don't know a thing about it."

"We could talk about you and Dad. Tell me about the time you brought in Dusty Green."

Dusty Green? Lord, did that name bring back memories. "Your father told you about Dusty, did he?"

"He said you saved the lives of three marshals that day."

"And just about lost my own."

"All four of you were trapped in Death Valley with nothing but the clothes on your backs and the blazing Nevada sun. You were out of food, running low on water, and had lost two horses to the coyotes, while not two hundred yards away sat Dusty Green and his gang, slurping down water and waiting for the four of you to surrender."

"Who's supposed to be telling this story?"

"After three days you were all determined not to be taken alive. You'd kill yourselves before you gave up. Matches were drawn, and Dad got the short one. He would be responsible for shooting the rest of you and then taking his own life."

Max gave her a stunned look. To the best of his recollection, Ed James had stretched the truth just a tiny bit. They'd been holed up on a sandstone ridge for three days after being ambushed by Dusty Green and his men. They were half starved and badly dehydrated. Hal Jones and Jimmy Muldone were close to unconsciousness. But actually, the short match had been responsible for the seemingly pointless task of watching over the two remaining horses on what the four of them had assumed would be their last night alive.

"And then you volunteered to sneak into the outlaw camp, full of fifty men, to steal their horses and supplies."

The number of men had been more along the lines of ten, but Max wasn't going to quibble now. "I was an idiot."

"But you succeeded."

"Luckily."

"And then you and Dad carried the two other marshals, who by this time were unconscious, to the nearest town."

Max fought down a laugh. And he supposed he and Ed had carried the two remaining *horses* as well?

"I love that story," she went on. "I never realized you were so young at the time."

"I was nineteen. And pretty damn full of myself."

She laughed. "Apparently not much has changed over the last ten years."

He gave her a glare. "I seem to recall your father remarking some ten years ago that his daughter wouldn't quit chasing boys around the schoolyard. Might I assume, judging by her history, that she never really stopped?"

"That was uncalled for. Two fiancés in two years doesn't make me promiscuous."

"Well, it certainly doesn't connote restraint."

"I'll thank you to keep your opinions to yourself."

"And I'll thank you to do the same."

A silence marked the sudden tension between them, and then Samantha said, "So much for that attempt at a civil conversation."

"We should have stuck with the bustle."

She started to laugh, and, despite his earlier irritation with her, Max found himself smiling.

10

Zack Strickland pushed his way up to the bar and plopped himself down on a stool. He ordered a bottle of whiskey and peered around the saloon from beneath his floppy hat. He'd followed his prey here to Spokane Falls. He could almost smell Max Barrett's scent, could almost feel the marshal's sticky blood on his hands.

The bartender dropped a bottle and a glass in front of him.

"I'm lookin' for a feller. A big man by the name of Barrett."

The barkeep shook his head and moved away.

"Did you . . . did you say Barrett?"

Strickland turned and narrowed his eyes on the dark-haired young man sitting next to him. "Yeah. Barrett. You know him?"

The man snorted drunkenly. "I know him," he said. "Ssstole my—ssstole my woman right out from under my nossse."

"You know where he is now?"

"He left! Headed off through the mountainsss—with my woman!"

The barkeep moved back in front of them and leaned over the bar. "Quiet down, Duncan. You disturb my customers and I'll toss you outta here on your ear."

The man named Duncan waved his hand. "Ahh, ssshhhut up."

"Where were they headed?"

Duncan squinted and blinked as though he'd forgotten who was sitting next to him. "Who?"

"Barrett. The man who stole your woman. Where's he headed?"

Duncan belched. "Utah. . . . Logan, Utah. Ssshe wantssa be a teacher!"

Strickland tugged at his beard. Barrett was leading a woman through the mountains? He broke into a smile. Nothing slowed a man down more than a woman.

"When'd they leave?"

Duncan was shaking his head. "Ssshe ssshouldn't a'left me. I'd a'done right by her."

Strickland was losing what little patience he had. He grabbed Duncan by the scruff of the neck and pulled his head back. "When did they leave?" he demanded into his face.

FAN THE FLAME 89

"Day . . . day before yesssterday."

He let go of Duncan's head and it dropped down to the bar with a thud. Barrett may have a two-day head start, but, with a woman along, he wouldn't be hard to catch. Logan, Utah. . . . Seemed he recalled having a cousin laying low in that area. He walked out of the saloon, and joined his two brothers who were waiting outside.

"Ya find him, Zack?"

"He's headed for Utah. Got himself a two-day start."

"Shit! Two days? Why the hell are you smilin'?"

"'Cause he's got a woman with him, that's why. And he's not just headed for Utah. He's headed for Logan, Utah."

Ben Strickland's eyes lit up. "Logan? Isn't—"

"That's right. All we have to do is send a telegram informing our loyal cousin that he's about to have guests." Zack laughed. "This is gonna be as easy as catching a two-legged rabbit."

Samantha stared into the embers of the campfire. She was two long days away from home and was missing her dad terribly. She was dirty and tired and lonely. And she was beginning to wish she'd never heard of Logan, Utah.

"Get some rest, Samantha."

She looked up at the man sitting across the fire from her. "I can't sleep."

"You look exhausted." He scrubbed his supper plate with a handful of dirt.

She listened to the night sounds of the forest around her, and a chill raced up her spine. Who knew what lurked just beyond the tree line?

"Tell me more about your family."

"Tell me more about yours."

"My mother died when I was five. My father retired soon after that. There's not much else to tell."

He stretched out on his side. "Then tell me about you."

"I grew up in Spokane Falls, played and fished in the river, climbed trees, hiked through the woods..."

"And you think that's typical, don't you?"

"Isn't it?"

"The young ladies I've known do not play and fish in rivers, they do not scramble up and down trees, and a hike through the woods would ruin their nails."

She fiddled with the edge of her blanket. "I suppose I'm uncultured."

"No. You're refreshing."

There was no mistaking the warmth in his eyes. She found herself relieved that he was stretched out a few feet away and not right next to her. "And they probably don't wear pants either?"

He smiled. "They don't have the legs for it."

She chewed at her lip. Was he complimenting her legs or insulting her odd style of dress? "But I'm sure they wear beautiful silk and lace dresses with parasols and a hundred petticoats . . ."

"That's to hide the hundred pounds of extra flesh packed into their corsets."

His smile became a full-fledged grin, and Samantha broke into laughter.

"Don't laugh, Miss James, I heard a man was killed last year by a corset that had blown its stays."

"I have to admit, I've never worn a corset."

His gaze drifted over her, and she suddenly felt hot all over, as if he'd physically touched her. "It would only get in the way of your silky skin."

The humor slipped from her face, and heat rushed up her neck.

His smile broadened once again. "We could light the town of Boston with that blush."

"You shouldn't say things like that to me."

"Because it makes you uncomfortable?"

"Because it isn't polite."

He rolled onto his stomach and in doing so edged a little close to her. "Complimenting you isn't polite? That's a new one to me."

Samantha was getting more and more flustered. "That wasn't a compliment, that was an assumption. You have no idea whether my—whether my skin is . . ."

"Whether your skin is silky?"

He was still grinning at her in that infuriating way. She clamped her lips shut and stared at the fire.

"You forget, Miss James, our kiss of only three nights ago. I recall touching quite a bit of you then."

He was so close, too close for her peace of mind. "You promised—"

"I promised I wouldn't take advantage of you. We're only having a discussion. I haven't even touched you. . . ."

Yet. She could have sworn he was going to say yet. She sat up quickly and scooted back into her bedroll. "I'm suddenly very tired, Mr. Barrett." She forced out a yawn. "I'll see you in the morning."

She thought she heard him chuckle as he found his own bed, but soon the only sounds were the crackling of the fire, the chirping of the crickets, and the pounding of her own heart.

11

Samantha slapped at the mosquito that was buzzing in her face. The late afternoon sun hung in front of her eyes, too low for the brim of her hat to offer any protection against its glare.

She squinted into the distance, looking for any sign of water. It had been two long days since she'd taken a bath in the stream. But this morning the marshal had promised her a bath, not just a wipe with a damp cloth. They would reach the Salmon River by nightfall.

They were traveling across a low mountain range, where the days grew warm and the nights quickly turned cold. Just to the west of them lay the Washington-Oregon border, to the east loomed the majestic Rockies.

She admired Max Barrett a great deal, she realized, looking at the solid line of his back as he rocked in his saddle ten feet in front of her. He was a man of determination and courage. His career alone proved that. And with every day she trusted him just a little bit more.

As they traveled along silently, she found herself focusing on his strong hands gripping the reins, and suddenly she had the overwhelming desire to feel his palms skim across her back, hear his breath whisper against her neck, taste his firm mouth. The long days were getting to her, and in the weary monotony of their journey she was finding it hard to control her wandering thoughts.

"There it is," Max called over his shoulder.

They approached a rocky beach where the river swirled in a deep tidal pool.

"You can take the first bath." He dismounted, led his horse behind a row of tall rocks, and sat down.

She watched with dawning shock as he leaned back against a large rock, unholstered his gun, and checked the cylinder. "You don't think I'm going to bathe with you sitting right there?"

He gave her a very serious look. "Grab the soap and a towel and go to it."

"I am not going to bathe with you sitting so close by, Mr. Barrett."

"Yes you are, Miss James. I'll stand guard for you and you'll stand guard for me. That's the way it's going to be or you won't bathe, period. Let us not forget your interesting run-in with the Indian our second day out."

Samantha glanced back at the water. If there was one thing in the world she wanted more than anything else right now it was a bath. "All right. But you keep your back turned."

It was difficult at first, taking off her clothes with a man so near. Her hands shook as she undid each of the buttons on her filthy shirt and pants. But the moment the water touched her dirty skin her apprehensions were washed away with the current.

The water was ice cold but heavenly. The pool was clear blue, and the bottom was covered with smooth rocks. She lathered her hair with the bar of soap.

"Everything all right?" she heard Max call from his place behind the boulder. She could just see a gray piece of his sleeve sticking out from the side of the rock and his shadow stretching long across the beach.

"Almost finished."

She sat down on the bottom of the deep pool and dunked her head underwater to wash the soap out of her hair. When she came back to the surface something slithering caught her eye. She let out a sharp scream.

Max leapt out from behind the rock, his gun leveled in Samantha's direction. He was going to kill whoever it was that had made her scream like that.

She screamed again, this time pointing a finger at him. "You said you'd keep your back turned!"

He quickly turned in the other direction. "For Christ's sake, what the hell made you scream?"

"There—there's a snake in the water. I saw it swim in—there it is!" He could hear her smacking at the water.

He backed toward the bank, looking over his shoulder, careful not to get her in his line of vision. "I don't know how you expect me to kill the damn thing if I can't even see where the hell I'm going!" He could hear her splashing around behind him, trying to get the snake away from her.

"Goddammit ta hell." He spun around and strode into the water. "The damn thing could bite you before I even get there!"

He walked right up to her, grabbed the slithering thing, which, as fate would have it, was a harmless grass snake, and flung it through the air.

Then he made the mistake of looking down at Samantha. She was crouched in the water, her hair hanging over her shoulders in dripping tendrils. Water beaded on the arms that she had crossed over her breasts.

His mouth went dry. "I don't suppose I could start my bath now?"

Her lips quivered, and he wanted to tug on them with his teeth.

"If—if you'll turn your back I'll—I'll get out and you can have the pool to yourself."

He gave her a lazy smile. Actually, he wouldn't have minded it a bit if she stayed. He pictured himself dropping to his knees, pulling her full breasts against him, and kissing her wet, sweet lips until she begged him for more. Cursing himself for making that damn promise to her father, he turned his back and listened to the sounds of her rising from the water.

The situation between them was only getting worse with time. How could he have believed that keeping her at arm's length would cool the attraction between them. If she'd only done as he'd hoped from the beginning and changed her mind about this trip . . . but regrets were beside the point now.

Here they were, with nothing but his blasted promise between them. How long could he resist her when she sat so enchantingly across the campfire from him every cold, lonely night? How long would he be able to control himself, waiting patiently behind a rock while she frolicked naked in a river? Maybe the real question was, how was she going to react when he broke his word and let his desire overcome his honor?

While the marshal bathed, Samantha put on a fresh dress and gathered small pieces of dried wood from the forest edge. The sun was almost setting, and the mountain would be getting cold soon.

She arranged the wood in a neat little teepee shape, struck a match, and soon had a blaze going.

When she looked toward the water her smile slipped from her face, the color draining from her cheeks. The marshal was approaching the bank in the waist-deep water, and he was completely bare, every muscular inch of him.

His finely sculpted naked chest filled her view. It was smooth and firm, and the sight of it made her eyes widen.

He seemed not to notice her gawking as he continued to move forward. When he was about to climb out she finally stopped him with a shout. "Wait! You don't have any . . . you're completely . . ."

He stopped and blinked, as if he'd just realized he'd been about to expose himself. "Sorry. Could you hand me that blanket?"

Samantha tore her eyes away from him long enough to reach for the blanket lying next to her on the ground. She stretched her arm out as far as it would go to offer it to him and then squeezed her eyes shut and turned her head away. When the weight of the blanket left her arm she knew the marshal was standing in front of her, bare except for a thin veil of dark brown wool.

"You can look now."

She opened her eyes and turned back to him, her stare focused again on his bare chest. "Don't you want to . . . to get dressed?"

"I drenched my only clean pair of pants saving you, Miss James." He had to have noticed her distraction, and he looked as if he were trying not to laugh. "I'd be awful cold sleeping in them, don't you think?"

"You'll catch cold like that," she responded, her throat suddenly gone dry.

"If you're really concerned about my warmth, you could join me under this blanket."

She looked up at him. His eyes were sparkling with laughter.

"I'm sure the fire will suffice."

"But it won't be nearly as much fun."

He sat down next to her, just a breath away, and began chewing on a tough strip of jerky. She just couldn't seem to keep her eyes off his smooth, broad chest, and kept stealing glances at him out of the corner of her eye.

"I don't suppose you'd like to touch it?"

She averted her eyes. "You shouldn't go around half dressed like that," she said in a weak voice. "What would you do if *I* sat at the fire with only a blanket wrapped around *my* waist?"

She realized what she'd said when his face lit up with a broad smile. "Well, I don't know. Maybe we should try it."

"My dad would call this a perfect example of fanning the flames in an already touchy situation."

He leaned closer. "But in order for there to be a flame, Sam darlin', first there has to be a spark." His eyes captured hers. "I don't suppose there's a spark flickering for me somewhere inside that sweet little heart of yours? One that kicks smoke in your eyes and makes it hard to see straight?"

His voice lowered, and he raised a warm hand to graze the side of her neck. "Does it clog your throat and make it hard to breathe? Would that spark catch if I just blew on it a little?"

He moved closer to her, and she was powerless to do anything but close her eyes and wait. She couldn't think of anything except how his firm chest was going to feel beneath her fingers.

A loud noise came from the trees, and they jumped apart as a pair of riders broke into camp. Marshal Barrett had the gun that he always kept beside him drawn from its holster before Samantha even knew what was happening.

"Hold on now," one of the men said. The stranger moved into the light of the fire with his hands raised.

"We saw yer fire from a distance and was hopin' you could share it with some fellow travelers," the other one said. They both climbed down from their horses.

The marshal kept his gun leveled on them and smiled. "Sure." He waved his pistol at the fire. "Help yourselves to some jerky."

The first one, who was blond, smiled back hesitantly. "Well, sir, we ain't gonna feel too welcome if'n there's a gun in our faces all evenin'."

The marshal smiled again, but Samantha read the mistrust on his face. "Of course." He laid his gun next to him on the ground and wrapped an arm around her shoulders.

She didn't resist, sensing that Marshal Barrett knew exactly what he was doing. The two men sat down at the fire across from them and began to gnaw on the jerky. "Where you folks headed?" the dark one asked.

"Nevada," the marshal replied.

"That so?" the blond one responded. "You folks Mormons?"

The man was eying Samantha carefully, sending a chill down her spine. She shivered, and Barrett pulled her closer. "This here is my only wife," he answered. "I don't think we fit the criteria."

"Well, you've got a right pretty wife, mister." The dark one's eyes raked over Samantha from across the fire. "It must be nice to have her with ya on chilly nights."

Marshal Barrett didn't respond. Samantha could sense the tension building within him.

"Don't suppose you'd be willin' to share?" the blond man said.

Samantha sat up straight. "I beg your pardon?"

"Ooh-wee, Randy," the blond one said, laughing softly. "She gots her some spunk."

Good Lord, Samantha thought. *Not another Randy.* "And she gots her a long knife in her boot," she replied.

"I don't think my wife wishes to be shared." Marshal Barrett lifted his gun and pointed it at the two men. "And, on second thought, maybe you two should go look for companionship elsewhere."

"Up here in these mountains it pays to be a bit more on the friendly side, mister."

"You'd do best to remember that," the dark one added.

The marshal smiled coldly. "Ride on out."

The two men stood and mounted their horses. Marshal Barrett watched them leave, and Samantha let out a breath of relief. "Randy. There must be a curse on the darn name."

The marshal stood and pulled her to her feet. "I want you down behind that boulder." He pointed toward the largest boulder on the bank and waited for her to comply.

Not understanding, she still did as she was told and crouched down behind the rock while trying to figure out what was going on. She didn't have long to wonder before a shot rang out, ricocheting off of a smaller rock close beside her. She stifled a scream of surprise and looked a few feet away to see the marshal crouched behind another rock. He had his gun out and was peering through the dark, trying to pinpoint their attackers.

"Just give us the woman," Samantha heard a voice echo.

The marshal shot her a glance, as if it were necessary to warn her to remain where she was. She crouched lower, ignoring the ache building in her tired legs. Another shot rang out, this time clipping the edge of the boulder where the marshal was hunched down.

Chips of rock flew through the air, and Samantha let out a loud gasp. "You boys are messin' with a United States Marshal!" she cried out.

The shooting stopped, and faint murmurs came from the trees. Samantha gave the marshal a triumphant smile, sure that she'd frightened the men off.

"My daddy was killed by a marshal down in Reno!" a man shouted, and then the shooting recommenced.

Marshal Barrett gave her an exasperated look, and Samantha ducked back down behind the rock where she belonged.

"I know you boys don't want me to kill ya," he called out. "I'm a damn fine shot. Never miss a thing I'm aiming at."

Despite the dire situation, Samantha had to smile. There Marshal Barrett was, dressed in nothing but a blanket, trying to sound tough and dangerous to two armed men.

He took a quick peek above his rock and fired. A scream of pain came from the woods. "He got me, Randy. Goddammit, he got me." The clatter of horses' hooves was heard a few moments later.

"I think they're gone," Samantha whispered.

"Well of course they're gone, Miss James. They are simply terrified of my profession."

She blanched at the sound of anger in his voice. "I was only trying to help."

"Announcing myself as a marshal usually does more harm than good, lady. So I'd appreciate it in the future if you'd just keep your mouth shut and do what you're told."

"That is the last time I ever try to help you!"

"Good! *You boys are messin' with a U.S. Marshal,*" he mimicked. "Christ!"

Samantha picked up his wet pants and threw them at him. They caught him around the face with a *splat*. She turned to get her bedroll and could still hear him grumbling on about what a "pain in the butt" she was.

"You're no prize yourself, you know! You think I'm having fun trudging through the wilds with a man who can't ride a horse and speak at the same time?"

"I'm not here for your enjoyment, lady, so forgive me if I forgo the juggling act."

"Would it kill you to keep up your end of a conversation every once in a while? I swear today I actually heard the trees growing!"

"That's surprising considering you never seem to close your mouth long to hear anything!"

She threw her bedroll down by the fire. "You

ungrateful lout. I wish you had put on those wet pants—and caught a hell of a cold!"

He paused in laying out his own bed. "You want entertainment, sweetheart? Here you go." Without warning he yanked the blanket off his bare hips and stood with his back to her in the moonlight, just long enough to give her a good look. Then he wrapped himself up in a dry blanket. "That oughta make for good conversation tomorrow." He lay down on his bedroll and promptly fell asleep.

Samantha didn't need the fire or her bedroll to keep her warm that night. The indelible memory of Max Barrett's bare backside was enough to keep her warm through a lifetime of winters.

12

Tommy and Randy Harris stumbled into the circle of firelight, the smell of burnt beans and weak coffee invading their noses. Randy helped his brother down onto an old tree stump. Tommy had his right hand clamped firmly to his bloody left arm. "That son-of-a-bitch hit me right in the gun arm."

Three pairs of yellow eyes peered at them from across the campfire.

"You never let on just how possessive he was about the woman," Randy said.

"Well wha'd ya expect, ya jackass!" Tyler Strickland burst out and then looked to his older brothers for approval. "He ain't about to give up a purty little thing like that easily. Right, Zack?"

Zack Strickland sat hunched over his coffee cup,

the orange glow of the fire gleaming in his eyes. His broad shoulders strained at his worn cotton shirt and leather vest. The two smaller men across the fire swallowed as the red-haired giant stared them down through the slits of his eyes.

"I told you to sneak in after dark and take her." He didn't even blink, although the heat and smoke from the fire would burn any normal man's eyes. "You've made my job a helluva lot harder, boys."

"W-well he done told us they was headin' for Nevada," Randy stammered.

Zack dumped the remaining contents of his tin mug into the dirt. "Then he lied. Now tell me somethin' I don't know."

Randy looked at his brother. They should have never offered to help these men, but a little liquor and some money waved around could always turn their heads. "H-he d-didn't tell us nothin' else, M-Mister Strickland," Tommy answered. He tightened his grip on his bloody arm.

Zack nodded and pursed his lips. He stuck a finger in his ear and wiggled it around. "This man killed my brother, boys. *Dead!*" he added with a roar. He moved back and forth in front of the fire, his large body blocking out everything behind him. "I ask you to do me one favor, *and you fucked it up!*" he bellowed again.

Then he unholstered his gun and shot a hole clean through the front of Tommy's head.

Randy watched in shock as his brother fell

backward to the ground. His knees began to shake, and sweat poured into his eyes. "P-p-please, M-Mister Strickland, sir." He shook his head as the gun was directed toward him. "W-we did the best we could."

Zack Strickland fired the next shot with a grin spread across his hairy face. "I always love it when they beg."

Samantha sat straight up in her bedroll, the sound of the shot still ringing in her ears. "What was that?" she asked, her voice shaking.

The marshal was awake and looking around them. "It came from a ways off."

Another shot rang out, and Samantha jumped. "I don't suppose it might be hunters?"

"In the dark?"

"What do we do?"

"We move ourselves very quietly, and very carefully, out of here."

Samantha was up and tying her bedroll to the back of her saddle before the tingle of sleep had left her head. Somebody was out there, shooting in the dark, and she saw no problem with moving on quickly.

The marshal pulled on his damp pants and stood up to pack his bedroll. "You ready?"

"All set."

He looked pointedly at her long skirt. "We have

to cross the river, you know. That's gonna get wet."

"Then I suppose I'll end up damp like you." She moved to mount her horse.

"You could take it off, stay clean and dry. Only the legs of your bloomers would get wet, and that's a hell of a lot better than a wet, droopy, skirt."

"Are you suggesting that I remove my dress?"

"Oh, for Christ's sake, do whatever the hell you want. I'm only trying to make the ride easier for you." He slapped his gray hat onto his head and mounted up.

Samantha stood there, glowering at him.

"Look, either take the damn thing off or get on your horse. We don't have time to sit here and bicker like a couple of newlyweds."

"Turn around."

"It's as dark as pitch out here."

She crossed her arms. "Turn around."

Sighing, he turned his horse away from her, and Samantha slipped out of her skirt and shoes. She folded the skirt neatly and put it in her saddlebags with her dirty pants, then she climbed up onto her horse. "I'm ready now."

"Well hallelujah." He gave his horse a nudge and started toward the river with the pack mule.

Samantha's mount followed, and when her bare feet touched the icy water she couldn't hold back a quick curse. She didn't appreciate the marshal's soft laugh of satisfaction.

They rode past the calm tidal pool and into the deeper, rougher water. Before too long the horses were swimming, fighting the rough current that threatened to pull them downstream.

It was so dark, Samantha could hardly make out the marshal in front of her. The noise of the rushing water was almost deafening, and when she felt her horse begin to struggle beneath her she felt the first real pangs of fear. Her horse was losing the battle. The current was dragging them away.

"Mr. Barrett!" she screamed. "Max!" But the sound of the rapids drowned out her voice.

She clung to her horse. She couldn't see the marshal anymore, and she decided that she was going to survive this ordeal if only to flail him within an inch of his life. He hadn't given her any indication that the crossing would be so treacherous!

She sighed with relief when she felt her mare's hooves touch on the bottom of the opposite bank. She thanked God, and gave her horse its head as it brought her safely up onto shore.

But where on the bank was she? How far had she drifted from Marshal Barrett?

In the distance she heard the cry of a wolf, and shivers ran down her spine. She was alone, and in the middle of nowhere.

The wind whipped through the trees, threatening to put out the modest campfire that lay nestled between several small rocks. Samantha sat on the hard ground, her hands jammed between her tightly clenched knees, buried in folds of the wool skirt she'd put on over her damp bloomers. The sun had yet to rise, and she had yet to see any sign of Marshal Barrett.

After waiting for him on the bank for hours, trying to remain calm as she listened for the sound of his horse, she'd decided on a fire. Surely he would smell the smoke and come in her direction.

It had been hard to find dry fuel for the tiny blaze, since the ground was covered with a heavy morning dew. But she'd been lucky to find the matches at the bottom of her saddlebags still dry, despite the wet crossing.

She fought the tears that threatened to blur her vision. She would be brave, and she would be strong. The marshal was bound to find her. She wiped her eyes with the backs of her hands and looked off to her left, through the trees, to watch the sun creep slowly over the horizon. Hadn't the fool man noticed her absence yet!

He couldn't be mad enough at her to leave her behind. She'd only been trying to help him the night before. Certainly he wouldn't hold that against her.

No, Marshal Barrett had promised that he would protect her, and, angry or not, he was a man of his word. He would come for her. She could only hope that he'd find her before some wild animal did.

Then she heard a new sound, the sound of something moving through the water on the other side of the dense trees that blocked the river from her view.

A horse's nicker reached her. She stood up relieved, brushing the dirt from her backside. "It's about time, Barrett," she whispered.

Sunlight filtered into the sky above her as she watched the trees, waiting for the marshal to emerge. Her tongue itched with the remarks she was going to throw at him. Had he known the river would be that deep and that swift? Had this all been disciplinary action on his part, to repay her for interfering in his shootout the night before?

When a large red-headed man stepped through the trees Samantha gasped. And when his face broke into a wicked leer she spun around and ran.

He chased her and caught her by the back of her skirt. She fell down, face first. He pulled her to her feet, and she screamed, loud and long.

The man clamped his hand over her mouth. "You holler like that again and I'll slit yer throat, you hear me!" His eyes darted around her camp. He lifted his hand from her mouth. "Where's your marshal friend?"

She shook her head.

He gave her a hard shake. "Tell me where he is!"

"I don't know," she cried. "We got separated crossing the river!"

He looked around the camp again. "You better be tellin' me the truth, sugar, or I'm gonna cut you up into tiny pieces and feed you to the fishies."

She swallowed down her fear. "I swear . . . I swear it's the truth."

He set her back from him. "Well, now. I suppose we'll have to wait for him to find ya then, won't we. In the meantime . . ."

He reached for her, and Samantha darted out of his grasp. "Who are you? What do you want?"

"Right now what I want is a nice piece of you. Come here. Come here to ol' Ben."

He lunged for her, and Samantha brought her knee up to the vulnerable spot between his legs. He doubled over but knocked her to the ground just the same. She tried to scramble away and put the campfire in between them, but he yanked her back to her feet and slapped her, hard, across the face.

"You fight me, bitch, and I'll fight you right back!"

Her jaw was throbbing from his blow. His hands began to roam over every inch of her body, squeezing and poking and prodding. She held down the bile rising up in her throat and tried not to breathe as he bit the tender skin of her neck. He was working her dress off of her shoulders and licking her ear.

Samantha heard the gunshot as if from a great distance. Her head had begun to swim, but the red-headed man crumbling at her feet brought her back to her senses. Not understanding what had happened, she turned around and ran.

She landed in Marshal Barrett's arms. She didn't have to see his face to know it was him. A sense of comfort and safety filled her, and she grabbed his shirt so he wouldn't disappear.

"Are you all right?"

She nodded her head, afraid to look back at the man lying on the ground behind her. "Who . . . who is he?"

He gently pushed her away from him. "Let's find out."

She watched as the marshal approached the prone man. Blood was spreading across the front of the man's dirty white shirt.

"Strickland," she heard Barrett mutter. The marshal's head came up, his eyes darting around the clearing and peering through the trees.

"Do you know him?"

He came back to her. "Get on your horse."

"Who—"

"Get on your goddamn horse!" He picked her up and practically dropped her into the saddle.

He mounted his own horse and, taking her reins, led her into the thick woods at a fast trot. She held onto the saddle horn and, glancing around, realized they didn't have their pack mule.

"Where's the mule?" she called to him.

"Gone."

"Gone?"

"I left it to look for you."

"We're not going to just leave it—"

"Why the hell did you light that damn fire!"

"It was a signal fire."

"No! You should have just sat your butt down and waited for me!"

She didn't understand what was making him so angry. "Waited for you to wander right past me?"

"If you'd stop doing so many stupid things it would make my job a helluva lot easier!"

"You're the one who made me cross that damned river! Why didn't you tell me it was so dangerous?"

"That *damned* river runs clear across this state. Unless you planned on a mighty big detour it was the only way to go!" He waited for her horse to come up beside his, and then he tossed her the reins. "Now shut your mouth, Miss James. Shut your mouth and stay directly behind me."

"It's not my fault that man attacked me!" She felt new tears forming. "I tried to run from him, but he—he grabbed my skirt and he—"

The marshal reached out and cupped the side of her face. She stared at him, feeling lost and confused. "I know it's not your fault, Samantha. But I've gotta get you out of here before the rest of that gang finds us. They must have followed me all the way from Billings."

"What are you saying?"

"I'm saying I've got a bloodthirsty gang on my trail, and I've just killed another member of their family. And if we don't get out of here fast, we're going to be coyote bait. I can't protect you and watch my back at the same time."

"Someone's after us?"

He ignored her question. "We'll zigzag through the trees so they'll have trouble finding our trail. In a day or so, we'll have outridden them."

"And if we don't?"

"Trust me."

She wanted to. She wanted to throw herself into his arms and bury herself against him where she'd be safe and warm, protected by his strength. "Do I have any other choice?"

"Stay close."

He kicked his horse and took off at a gallop through the trees. Samantha stayed so close to him that if he'd stopped too fast she would have been riding his horse.

13

Samantha sat on the cold ground within a stand of tall pines. She was wrapped in a wool blanket and chewing on a tough strip of jerky. The higher they climbed into the mountains the colder it got. Her breath was a fog on the frigid night air.

Along with the pack mule they'd lost all their food supplies and just about everything she owned. She'd spent yet another long day in the saddle only to end up in a cold camp for the night. Although she understood the marshal's reasoning for not wanting to build a fire, this one final inconvenience had sent her into a bear of a mood.

"This tastes like shoe leather," she said.

"It's better than nothing, Miss James."

"It *is* nothing, as far as I'm concerned. How are we supposed to live like this? No fire, no food, no clean clothes."

He was sitting across from her with his rifle across his lap. All she could see was the glow of his clear blue eyes in the moonlight. "We'll make do."

"How? Without a fire we can't cook anything we might be lucky enough to catch. We're going to starve to death if we don't freeze to death first."

"We won't freeze, Miss James. Not with all that hot air flying out of your mouth."

She hauled back her arm and threw her jerky at him. "You're supposed to be protecting me, and you're going to end up getting me killed!"

"If you don't keep your voice down I might kill you myself."

"I can't believe my father trusted you. Not only am I in danger of losing my life, but it's all because of you!"

He lunged forward and clamped his hand over her mouth. He tasted like dirt and sweat. "What do I have to do to keep you quiet? I can understand that you're afraid, Miss James, but now is not the time to get bitchy."

Bitchy?

She bit into his palm, and he sat back with a yelp and a murderous glare.

"If I die out here I'm going to haunt you for the rest of your life, Mr. Barrett. And if I get so lucky as to take you to the grave with me, you'll have no trouble finding me in heaven. I'll be the one slamming the pearly gates in your face!"

There was a moment of silence as he crouched in

front of her, staring as if he were contemplating something dire. "What are you thinking?" she demanded.

"That if I shove my tongue down your throat you might shut the hell up."

She gasped. "And if I don't lose my jerky all over the front of your shirt in response, I'll bite your tongue clean off!"

"It's hard to moan and bite down at the same time."

"There's a big difference between a moan and a scream."

"You scream and we'll be having the Stricklands over for supper."

"Maybe after a fistful of this jerky they'll fall down dead!"

He sighed. "If we ride hard and fast we can reach Logan within seven days. Between now and then there will be no fires, no impromptu baths, and no screaming. You will stay within reach of me at all times, that includes at night, and you will do exactly what I say without hesitation."

There was a long pause. "Is this where I'm supposed to say, 'Yes, Sire, king of all the lawmen?'"

He picked up his rifle and dropped down beside her on the oiled canvas of her bedroll. "Your sarcasm is beginning to chap my ass, Miss James."

She arched a brow. "You can still feel yours?"

He reached for his blankets and began spreading them out over both their legs.

"What are you doing?"

"Trying to keep you warm so you'll live to torment me another day. Take off your boots."

She couldn't believe he was bold enough to try something like this. And after the promise he'd made to her father! "I most certainly will not."

"Look, lady, I'm not going to have my legs bruised up by the heels of your boots. Take the things off."

"I am not sleeping with you," she said. "So whether I leave them on or not should make little difference."

He threw back the blanket and pulled her foot into his lap. She struggled with him and opened her mouth to scream, but he gave her the most vicious glare she had ever seen in her life. "You make one sound and so help me I'll tie you to a tree and leave you there to rot. You don't seem to understand, Miss James. These men that are after me, they won't just shoot me and let you go. They'll beat you, rape you, and kill you. Not necessarily in that order. Without a fire, we could both die of hypothermia in our sleep. The heat from our bodies could very well be the only thing to keep us both alive tonight. So what's it gonna be? Death . . . or me?"

He looked as if he were about to kill her with his bare hands, and for a brief moment Samantha thought she would get the former no matter what her decision. Pulling her leg off his lap, she yanked off both her boots, bound herself up in her warm blanket, and flopped down onto her side, facing away from him. There. She hoped he was happy.

"Give me the blanket."

She looked over her shoulder at him. "What?"

"We have to share heat, Miss James. Your blanket is going to prevent that from happening."

"Mr. Barrett, I am perfectly warm."

"In one hour you're going to be shaking from head to toe."

He took hold of one edge of her blanket and unrolled her. She landed with her nose against his chest, and he held her there with one hand while he spread four heavy blankets over them. The last blanket he pulled up high over their heads, and then he molded her tightly against him in the circle of his arms. He caught one of her knees between his legs, and tucked her feet under his.

Samantha felt warmer than she'd been in days and more tense than she'd been in her life. Without the moon shining on his face she could no longer see his eyes, but she could feel his hot breath against her forehead. She stole a peek up in the direction of his face.

"Get some sleep, Miss James."

She relaxed a little. "What if they . . . what if they find us while we're asleep?"

He rubbed her back, and she stiffened, until she realized his action had been involuntary. "They can't find us in the dark any easier than we can find them. The horses will warn us if anybody gets too close."

A few moments of silence passed in which Samantha heard his breathing growing loud and even. "Mr. Barrett?" she whispered.

"What?"

The fact that he'd answered her so clearly surprised her. "I . . . I just wanted to know if you were asleep."

"I'm not."

"I thought maybe you were."

"Well, I wouldn't be *now,* would I."

"Listen, could . . . could you do me a favor?"

"Ask."

"Could you let me fall asleep first? I hate being out here alone, and I feel like the last person on earth when you fall asleep before I do."

He settled in closer to her. "I know that feeling."

"Then you'll stay awake until you know I've gone to sleep?"

"I suppose I can manage it if you start now."

Samantha smiled and curled her fists between her and his chest. "Oh, and Marshal?"

"Hmmm?"

"I'm sorry I got bitchy."

"I know you are, Samantha."

14

Despite the coldness of the early spring evening, Samantha felt sweat trickle down between her shoulder blades. She was wrapped up in Max's warm coat, her back ached, her ribs hurt, the muscles in her thighs were in knots, and her head was pounding.

The last five days had been miserable. They'd ridden relentlessly, watching every tree, every bush, every rock large enough to hide a man. At night they slept huddled together, warding off the cold, talking about anything that popped into their heads, and arguing just to keep things interesting. They'd fallen into a routine of mounting up before sunrise, speaking little on the trail, riding until dark, and then falling into bed exhausted every night. They never slept for very long, and the combination of fatigue and hunger was really starting to get to Samantha.

She rubbed her aching head with gentle fingers. As the sun finally began to drop in the sky, marking the end of another day's ride, she didn't care if the Strickland brothers found them or not. She was just too damn tired to care. Let them come and put her out of her misery.

Her horse came to a sudden stop, and she looked up. The marshal showed no visible symptoms from their week-long strain. He had paused at the top of a rise, looking down upon a small valley. Below them, nestled safely between the hills, lay a large homestead with smoke pouring from its stone chimney.

"Now that looks inviting," Max said.

She urged her horse up next to his. The temperature was falling rapidly, and their breath was already beginning to form a fog.

She stared at the home with longing. How her bones ached for the comfort of a soft bed, how her stomach yearned for the fulfillment of a satisfying meal. "Do you suppose they might take us in?"

His blue eyes settled on her, and even in her cold, miserable state Samantha felt her heart lurch. "We've just crossed into Utah. Chances are they're Mormon."

"For all I care there can be fifty wives to one man in that house. I just want a soft bed and a hot, tasty meal."

He turned toward her, looking indecisive. "I don't suppose it would hurt to ask. Let's see how friendly they are."

The pain in Samantha's head began to ease as she followed Max's horse down the steep hill. For almost an entire week she'd been without common comforts, without the taste of decent food in her mouth, and, even though the sun shone brightly throughout the day, she'd had a feeling that she would never feel warm again. She was having a hard time not leaping from her horse now and running the rest of the way to the house.

When they reined up in front of the neat, large, log house, Max dismounted first. He undid his holster and slipped his gun into the back of his pants beneath his jacket. Then he raised his arms to Samantha.

She eased one stiff leg over the pommel and fell into his arms. Resting her hands on his strong shoulders, she slipped to the ground, her breasts tingling as they skimmed against his chest. He drew in his breath, and she took a step back.

"Shall we?" she asked.

He climbed the two wooden steps to the front door and knocked loudly. She moved up next to him and listened expectantly for sounds of movement inside.

The door creaked open slowly, and the face of a black-bearded man peeped through the crack. "Yes?"

Max took off his hat. "The name's Barnes, sir. Max Barnes. And this here's my wife, Samantha." He draped one of his arms around her shoulders.

"We was just passin' by and couldn't help but see the lights and the mighty welcomin' smoke a'billowin' from your chimney there. It's awful cold out here, sir. I was hopin' you might have a warm place for the wife and I ta stay the night."

The stern-faced man eyed the two of them. Samantha didn't like the idea that Max was lying to the man, but she wasn't about to raise a complaint if it got them into that warm, wonderful-smelling haven behind the door.

The man obviously decided that they were harmless, because his face suddenly broke into a wide grin. He swung the door wide. "The name's Hiram." He stuck out a skinny hand which Max promptly shook. "Get your wife in here and get yourselves warm."

When the door shut behind them the warmth of the home seeped into Samantha's cold body. The room they found themselves in was huge, and dominated by the largest kitchen table Samantha had ever seen. It was a good thing, for all around her stood at least fifteen children of every shape and size.

A warm fire blazed in the hearth against the far wall. A large black kettle rested in the fire's flames, cooking something that smelled suspiciously like chicken and dumplings.

The place was well lit, with lamps illuminating every dark corner. Colorful rag rugs covered the wooden floors, but chairs were limited in the sitting room. She assumed that most of the resting was done at the massive trestle table.

"Now, we don't want to inconvenience ya none." Max was still playing the part of a simple, humble man. "It's just that the wife and I've been travelin' for more than a week now, and, well, she's startin' to look a mite thin."

"Oh, my dear." Samantha looked toward the stairs and saw a woman with a sympathetic expression coming toward her. "You must be half frozen and half starved."

The woman took Samantha's hands and led her toward the stairs. "Caleb, Nephi, bring up the tub. Rachel, you and the girls heat up some water for the lady." The woman turned to Samantha. "We'll have you back to your old clean, warm self in no time."

Samantha gave Max a thrilled smile before she followed the woman up the steps. She was ushered into the last room at the end of a hallway and directed to sit on the softest feather bed she'd ever felt.

The woman stood above her, arms crossed, shaking her head. "You poor thing. Your husband is right. You do look bone thin."

Samantha glanced down at herself. She didn't think she was all that bad off.

Two tall boys entered the room, hefting a large, barrel-tub over their heads. As their mother gave them further orders, Samantha looked around the room.

As sparsely furnished as the rest of the house, it had only the necessary comforts: the large, incredibly comfortable bed, a long pine chest of drawers with a mirror above it, and a scattering of rag rugs similar to those she'd admired downstairs.

Four young girls filed in, each carrying a steaming bucket, and they emptied the hot water into the tub.

"Now fetch two of cold, Rachel."

"They're charming children," Samantha said, smiling as the girls curtsied and left the room.

The woman stared after them with a proud smile on her face. "They are not all mine. The two eldest boys, Caleb and Nephi, are Mary's children." She turned to Samantha. "I am Sarah. And you are?"

"Samantha." She rose from the bed. "We're so grateful that you've taken us in like this."

"We are all God's children, Samantha, brothers and sisters to each other. Would you not take in your brother or sister if they came to your home in need?"

Samantha nodded. The Mormons' ideas might seem strange to some, but their hearts were definitely in the right place.

"Just the same, thank you, Sarah."

The girl named Rachel brought in two buckets of cold water, retreated from the room, and closed the door.

Sarah turned back to her guest, eyeing her dirty

blue dress. "I believe I have something that might fit you." She lifted the buckets of cold water and added them to the hot in the tub. "This should do. Tonight I will wash your clothes and dry them by the fire. They will be ready for you by morning."

Samantha was shocked at the woman's generous offer. "You don't have to do that, Sarah. I can wash my own clothes."

Sarah smiled beatifically. "Nonsense. You are too tired to toil over your garments. I can take care of them for you."

She walked to the dresser and took out of the top drawer a towel and a round bar of soap. She handed the soap to Samantha. "It's perfumed with roses," she whispered with a gleam in her eyes. "I use it only on the nights I spend with Hiram."

This statement aroused Samantha's curiosity. Did it mean that Hiram spent the other nights with other wives, however many he had? How did it feel to know that the man you loved was in another woman's arms while you lay alone in your bed?

A vision of Max flitted through her mind, a vivid picture of him wrapped in the grasp of some long-limbed beauty, and a sharp pang of jealousy sank into her heart.

"Samantha? Are you all right?"

Samantha shook her head to come back to reality. "I must be very tired."

"I'll leave you now. Do you have all that you need?"

Samantha could only nod, her heart still thumping madly as Sarah left the room.

She peeled her clothes off her body, concentrating on the steam rising up from the tub. She refused to even consider what her heart was trying to tell her. She was just tired, that was all. After a good night's rest her sense would surely return.

15

Samantha sank low in the water with a long, drawn-out sigh. Her freshly washed hair ran free down her back. She lifted her feet, stretched her legs out on the far rim, and with her toes rubbed the lather that still clung to one of her ankles. Then she leaned her head back and dropped her wet arms over the edge of the wooden tub.

This was the image that greeted Max when he quietly entered the room. His breath quickened at the sight of her. The always persistent ache for her magnified to an agonizing degree, and he leaned back against the door, swallowing hard.

The lantern on the bedstand cast her incredible body in a soft glow. He stared at the long bare legs that stretched out on the rim of the tub, wanting only to part them and bring himself between their silkiness.

He heard a small shocked sound and a quick splash. His eyes darted from her legs to her face. She'd seen him, and by the look on her face she wasn't very happy with his intrusion.

She drew her legs down into the water. "What are you doing here?"

He smiled. "It seems your new friend Sarah thought you might want to bathe your husband when you were finished." His eyes strayed to the soapy water where her treasures were almost visible to his hungry eyes.

She pulled her knees up to her chest and glared at him. "You should've informed her that I would not be interested, and that you don't need a bath."

Now that they were safe, tucked warmly in this friendly house, Max finally allowed himself to feel the full desire for her he'd fought for the six long days he'd held her every night. He was too tired and too damn horny to play the valiant escort tonight. He'd given his word not to take advantage of Samantha on the trail. But this house was not the trail.

He moved toward the bed and tucked his gun under one of the pillows. Then he turned to Samantha.

"I think you've been in there long enough. Do I join you, or do you get your shapely bottom out?"

"If you want me out of this tub, Mr. Barrett, then you'd better get yourself out of this room.

I'm not going to parade around in front of you naked."

He crouched down by her face and dipped his hand into the water. His fingertips brushed against her thigh, and it took every ounce of willpower he possessed not to kiss her.

"It's getting cold, Samantha. Get out or I'll join you."

Samantha squeezed her arms tighter around her bent legs as if to ward off his approach. Max leaned closer, shortening the distance between their noses. He didn't denying himself a lingering glance down at the swell of her full breasts. "Need I count to three?"

Had he shocked her to silence? To his great delight, she wasn't moving.

He tipped his head and rubbed his moustache against the side of her cheek and began to count softly. "One . . ."

"Wait. H-hand me the towel."

He ignored her. "Two . . ."

He decided to make her wait for the number three. He took a lingering taste of her lips. She was soft and sweet, and he'd almost convinced himself to get in the tub, clothed or not, when a knock sounded on the door.

They both jumped. "Yes?" Max called.

"I was told to give this dress to Mrs. Barnes," said a tiny voice outside the door.

Max rose and opened the door.

"My mother was wondering if you had any clothes that needed washing, Mr. Barnes."

He was about to say no when Samantha, the woman who couldn't seem to utter a word moments ago, piped up, "Yes, he does. Why don't you get them for the girl, Mr. Barnes?"

Max gave her a scowl, and she smiled innocently. "I'll be back, Samantha. We'll continue our discussion then." He tossed the dress to her and left the room.

As soon as the door was shut, Samantha sprang from the tub. "Dear God, the man has lost his mind!" she whispered to herself while she struggled to pull the borrowed dress on over her damp body. She was determined to be out the door before Max returned to finish their "discussion." Unfortunately, no underthings came with the dress. Samantha would have to put up with the cool air blowing up between her legs. She brushed out her hair, pinned it up, and hurried downstairs for supper.

She sat rigidly at the table, her legs crossed tightly in front of her. Max sat next to her and insisted on rubbing against her whenever he so much as reached for the glass in front of him. She glared at him, earning herself one of his looks of mock innocence.

With determination she focused on the delicious meal in front of her.

"Your husband tells us you are journeying to Logan, in the Cache valley," Hiram said. "That is a good place to settle now that the Indian treaty is signed." He returned to eating his food.

"We won't be settlin' there, Hiram. I plan to take my wife a bit farther south . . ."

Although she knew Max was simply playing a role, his statement shook her to her toes.

" . . . Where we'll build us a proper home and have us a baby every year."

Samantha felt his hand squeeze her leg under the table. She uncrossed her legs and stomped on his foot, then smiled as he choked on his dumpling.

Sarah rose and began clearing the table. Samantha offered to help but the woman held up her hand. "No need to bother," she said. "You best get yourselves to bed if you plan on leaving early in the morning. We'll pack some food to take with you when you leave."

Samantha was once again amazed at the woman's generosity. "You're so very kind, Sarah."

Sarah smiled. "I hope you rest well, Sister Barnes."

Samantha felt the pressure of Max's arm as he helped her stand. "'Night everybody," he said, and guided her toward the stairs.

She looked at him in confusion and then, as realization dawned, tried to pull away.

He held her close to his side and whispered,

"We're husband and wife, remember? What are they going to think if we sleep in separate rooms?"

He didn't look like he was teasing. As a matter of fact, he looked nothing but sincere. What if the deeply religious family discovered that she and Max weren't married? Would they be put back out in the cold? Samantha knew she wouldn't be able to stand that, so she obediently climbed the stairs at Max's side.

Max closed the door to the room. He eyed Samantha appreciatively as she crossed the floor to the bed. She lifted the heavy, blue patchwork quilt and heaved it to the floor. A pillow followed. "You can sleep there."

He raised his brows and moved toward her. "I've been sleeping on the hard ground just like you, Miss James. I'm not sleeping on the floor."

"*I'm* not sleeping on the floor."

"You're more than welcome to join me in the bed."

Two bright splotches of red stained her cheeks. "I may have shared blankets with you on the trail—purely out of necessity—but I am not sharing that bed with you." She crossed her arms and tipped up her nose, giving him her best stubborn look.

Max shrugged and began unbuttoning his shirt. He slid it off his shoulders, watching Samantha's face carefully, but she remained determined to stare at the ceiling.

He took off his boots. His hands roamed to the buttons on his pants. One, two, three, four, he flicked each one open, still watching the enchanting beauty in front of him.

When he pulled his trousers away from his waist, he saw her eyes dart briefly in his direction, and he knew, whether she was looking or not, that he had her full attention. In one smooth motion his pants came off, and with them his under drawers. Then he walked, naked, to the bed.

She was still staring at the ceiling. "If you're trying to shock me, Mr. Barrett, it isn't going to work." Her arms were still crossed, but her foot was tapping madly.

Max climbed beneath the covers. After watching Samantha struggle not to look at him for a moment, he yanked back the blankets on the other side of the bed. "Join me?"

She braved a glance at him and flushed three shades of red. A heat started between Max's legs and began to spread throughout his body. He had to have this woman.

She looked down with longing at the spot in the bed beside him, and Max took note of her indecision. It seemed she needed an excuse. "This is the last bed you'll have until we get to your aunt's."

"You told me just this morning that it would

only be two more days before we reached Logan."

Max thought for a moment. "All right, Samantha, what if Sarah comes in to check on us in the middle of the night? She's a considerate woman. She may want to make sure we're warm enough in this drafty room. What's that chaste, Mormon woman gonna think when she sees Mrs. Barnes sleepin' on the floor? How do you think she'd view you if she knew that you were traveling with me, unmarried, unchaperoned?"

Samantha's hesitation lasted only a moment more. With the speed of light she dove under the covers and turned her back to him. "I would hate to have Sarah disappointed in me."

Max leaned up on one elbow and stared down at her. He shook his head. All she'd needed was the proper excuse.

He moved his hand to caress her and frowned when he realized she was still wearing a dress. "Are you sleeping in this?"

"I'm certainly not dancing in it." She yawned.

With a grunt, Max fell back to his pillow. He wished he had the violence in him to tear the damn thing off her. But what had he expected? That she'd fall into his bed and into his arms with a moan of ecstasy? She was an innocent and would have to be wooed, seduced.

With this in mind, he rose back up and leaned over her. He heard her deep, gentle breathing and shook his head, smiling wryly. His little sprite had fallen asleep.

One of her feet reached back and snuggled between his legs. He caught his hand up in her hair and fanned it out on the pillow above her head. It was going to be one hell of a long night.

16

Samantha yawned and opened her eyes to the bright sunlight of a new day. Birds were chirping outside, and a breeze was rustling through the trees. She smiled, closed her eyes, and burrowed into the soft bed. She'd never awakened feeling quite so warm, almost as if there were a fire burning right there in the bed with her.

Her eyes flew open, realizing it was no fire, but the burning pressure of Max against her back. His head was nestled into the base of her neck, and his even breathing blew gently across her shoulder. She was stunned to feel his hard body pressed against her.

During the course of the night her modest dress had ridden up to her waist. She was without underthings, and one of Max's strong hands was now riding intimately upon her bare hip. With a sharp breath, she realized just where one of his knees was nudging as it rested between her legs.

She noted the change in his breathing and knew he was awake. He caressed her slowly, sliding his hand down the length of her thigh. "Good morning," he murmured in her ear.

Tremors of desire shot through her, and she leaped out of bed in a flurry of discarded blankets. She turned back only to see the delighted smile on Max's face before he broke into laughter.

"I never realized you could move so quickly in the morning. I'll remember that the next time I have to rouse you out of our bedroll."

"A snake beneath the blankets would get anybody's attention."

"A snake?"

"You know, a slithery, slippery, slimy creature that makes its bed beneath other people's blankets?"

"I don't recall you waking up in such bad moods in the wild."

"Well, I don't recall ever having been groped in my sleep."

Now Max was frowning, but Samantha could deal with that. It was his charming smile that was always so unsettling.

"It was you who had your backside all snuggled up against me, sweetheart."

"I told you to sleep on the floor! Any decent gentleman would have!"

"Then I guess you're finally starting to see that I'm no decent gentleman. Anything else I can help you with?"

"Yes! Get your clothes on and get out!"

Max threw back the covers and rolled out of bed. His feet hit the floor, and Samantha's eyebrows hit her hairline. He was naked, all six foot five inches of him.

She couldn't look away, not this time. Her eyes grazed over the rippling planes of his back and slid down the powerful curve of his backside.

He turned to her, and she quickly raised her eyes to his face. The faint smile he was giving her was an obvious challenge, but she didn't have the courage to look further down.

"Your clothes, Mr. Barrett," she managed to say with some amount of control.

"What about my clothes, Miss James?"

"Put them on."

When she said "Put them on," she hadn't meant for him to slide into his drawers with a painstaking slowness, or for him to ease into his denims as he might slip into a warm soaky bath.

By the time he was working on the buttons the world had started teetering beneath Samantha's feet. She had to sit down on the bed or she'd fall down on the floor.

"You look hungry."

She looked up at him, his smile barely registering. She did feel a certain kind of hunger, one she knew couldn't be satisfied by food. She wanted him, the way a woman wants a man. Not even Randy had caused this sort of craving deep inside her.

Remembering Randy, Samantha's mind snapped back to reality. Randy had hurt her, cheated on her. Was she ready to put her heart on the line like that again?

Max was watching her carefully. "Would you like me to take them off and put them back on again?"

"I'd rather you left so that I could change."

He hesitated for a moment and then slipped on his shirt. "Don't take too long, we're wasting sunlight as it is."

Sarah knocked on the door a few minutes after Max left the room and handed Samantha the dress she'd been wearing the day before. She put it on, along with her freshly washed underthings, and met Max downstairs.

They mounted up before the dew had dried. After they thanked the family profusely and Samantha gave Sarah a promise to come back that way when she could, they rode off up the hill.

They kept their pace at a gallop for most of the day. Lunch was eaten in the saddle: jerky strips and some biscuits Sarah had packed for them. As usual their conversation was stilted as they trudged along.

Night couldn't have come quickly enough, as far as Samantha was concerned. The hot bath and soft, restful sleep the night before had spoiled her, and her newly jarred bones ached.

At camp, she dismounted from her horse, leaned back against its flank for a moment, and reacquainted her legs with solid ground. She watched the marshal untie his bedroll and spread it on the ground. She knew that, as on many nights before, they would have no campfire, for fear of attracting the Stricklands' attention. To stay warm, she would be sharing body heat with Max Barrett once again.

She stared at him apprehensively. After last night, she was no longer sure she could trust him to keep his word to her father.

"You know . . . it's not so cold tonight. I think I'll just take my own bedroll and sleep over here."

"Forget it."

His commanding response only hardened her resolve. "Mr. Barrett, after last night I refuse to share that bedroll with you."

"Forgive me, Miss James, did I miss something? Nothing happened last night."

"That's right—no thanks to you. Now give me my blankets."

Sighing, he shook his head. "Fine." He threw her the bedroll. "I'm too damn tired to fight with you over this tonight."

She spread her bedroll out beneath a tree, over a soft bed of pine needles, and bundled herself up in its warmth.

Sleep was a long time in coming. It was bitterly

cold. She hadn't realized just how much heat their two bodies could generate. And she not only felt cold, but lonely. After a full hour of battle to keep her toes warm, her fatigue won out and she floated off to a fitful sleep.

The chattering of her own teeth woke her. Her body was shaking all over. The moon was still high in the sky, and she knew that night still had a long way to go before morning took over.

Ducking her head under her blankets, she huddled into her meager shelter but continued to shake. She was going to freeze to death before the sun rose.

She lifted her head from the covers and looked around the dark camp. A brisk wind stung her nose and watered her eyes. She could barely make out the shape of Max in his bedroll, but, knowing that she was making the right decision, she drew her blankets around her shoulders and darted to his side.

"Mr. Barrett?" she whispered between chatters of her teeth. "Max!"

He opened one blue eye and stared up at her. "What?"

"I-I'm f-f-freezing."

He tossed aside a corner of his covers and pulled her in next to him. Soon they were both warm and toasty, and she quickly fell asleep against his chest, lulled by the familiar rhythm of his heartbeat and deep even breathing.

* * *

Max slept fitfully. His dreams were too real and too arousing to give him any rest.

Finally he opened his eyes and sensed Samantha's warmth immediately. He was sure she had opted to sleep alone that night, and he tried to remember just how she'd come to be all snuggled up against him. He pulled her closer and brushed a kiss against her forehead. She sighed but didn't wake.

He closed his eyes, determined to go back to sleep, but his hands, as if of their own will, started to roam the familiar frame in his arms. The sight of her in the bath the night before was coming back to him and, without thinking, he began unbuttoning the front of her dress.

He knew it wasn't right, not while she slept, so trusting, in his arms. But his desire for Samantha James had no moral conscience.

Carefully, he eased the dress off her shoulders.

He traced the smooth arch of her neck and dipped his fingers in the hollow of her shoulder blade. She was all honey and cream. He bent his head to taste her.

She stirred. "What are you doing?"

"You're cold. I'm warming you up." He nipped the tender skin beneath her ear.

"But you gave your word—"

He leaned on one arm, grasped her with his

free hand, and kissed her into silence. It felt good, great in fact, to forget for a while. To forget the fear he had that the Stricklands might find them before he got her to safety, to forget the impossible promise he'd made to her father to stay away from her.

He pulled back from her and lost himself in the shadows of her brown eyes. "My God, Samantha," he said. "I want you so badly. So badly."

Samantha shivered, but not because of the cold: Max's hands were heat enough for her. His warm sighs echoed in her ear as he ran his lips up and down her neck, making her heart flutter like the fragile wings of a hummingbird. She couldn't find the will to stop him as he pushed her dress to her waist.

"To hell with promises," he whispered. His lips grazed the sensitive skin of one of her breasts. "To hell with the world."

He licked her, sending a shock like pure lightning shooting up her spine. He ran a hand down the curve of her naked back and rested it on her hip before rolling, moving her beneath him. Her breasts felt on fire as they pushed against his hard chest.

He touched his nose to hers and ran his tongue along her lower lip.

She tried to calm her rapid breathing, tried to think straight, but she couldn't seem to concentrate on anything but him. She parted her lips to take a deep breath, and his warm, wet tongue slipped inside her mouth.

She swept her hands into his soft hair and mastered the rhythm he was setting with his mouth. Her hands moved down his neck to his shoulders, feeling every inch of muscle she'd seen that morning.

"Don't stop," she whispered.

"Oh, honey, I won't."

Like a velvet caress, he moved his hands over her sensitive body, building her appetite for him, and she cried out as he did a sweeping motion between her thighs with his fingers.

"You're ready for me, Samantha," he whispered. "As ready as I've been for a long time."

She heard his voice as if from a great distance. Once again those long incredible fingers of his were between her thighs and parting her legs. She widened her eyes as slowly, ever so slowly, a strange sensation began to form inside her.

Her body started to tremble as dawn touched her face, lighting up her eyes as a cry of ecstasy tore from her throat. She felt her flesh quiver beneath his fingertips, felt her muscles contract, felt herself break free of her mind as a vibrant heat stole through her body.

Max kissed her, lingeringly, then he slipped an arm beneath her bottom and brought her hips up to his. He buried himself inside her and groaned as she cried out from a brief stab of pain.

He paused above her for a moment. She ran her hands down the curve of his back.

"You promised you wouldn't stop," she said.

He groaned, and with long, penetrating strokes, brought them both to the edge.

He let out a low growl and sank himself deep inside her. He was taking her back toward the wave of ecstasy he'd sent her crashing through once before, his powerful body rising and falling above her.

Suddenly he stopped, his blue eyes locking with hers. "You're mine," he whispered.

And with one, final, potent thrust, she was.

17

The bright sun woke Max the next morning, and he looked down at the sleeping woman in his arms. Samantha's eyes were closed, her long, dark lashes lying softly against her cheeks, her pink lips parted in sleep. The faintest smile curved her mouth.

What the hell had he done?

He'd broken his promise to a man he admired and respected, and he'd stolen the virginity of a very decent woman, that's what he'd done. He could put the blame on Samantha and tell himself she'd tempted him until he could stand it no more, but the plain truth was he'd ached for her since he'd met her. Like an inexperienced schoolboy, he'd let the muscle between her legs rule over the giant space of air between his ears.

She was going to wake up and want things from

him, he knew it as surely as he knew snow melted, rivers ran, and sugar tasted sweet. First his promise to Ed, then the Stricklands, now this. It seemed that every day his life was getting a little more complicated.

She sighed in her sleep and turned her face against him. He looked back down at her, naked in his arms. He felt the heat of her skin, the curves of her bottom in his hands, and wanted her all over again. He turned his head away, knowing he couldn't let it happen. He'd have a hard enough time explaining to her his reasons for last night; he didn't need to make things worse by adding another interlude to the list.

Her hands moved over his hips and slipped around to his back. She was waking up, and he wanted to pull her mouth to his and plunder every little charm she had to offer.

Steeling himself against the cold air, he slipped his arms out from around her and eased up out of the blankets. She stirred but then went right on sleeping. He put on his clothes, washed his face in canteen water, and went into the bushes to take care of business.

Samantha suddenly opened her eyes. When she remembered the night before it was with a sting of embarrassment. The blankets beside her were empty. She stole a quick glance around the camp and caught sight of Max returning from the woods. Their eyes met, and she gave him a faint smile. Had she really lain here last night and made passionate love with this man?

The expression on the marshal's face did little to quiet her unease. He looked almost contrite as he approached her.

"Time to get up," he said, barely looking her in the eye as he turned to give the horses a handful of grain.

Samantha sat up, keeping the blankets over her naked body as she slipped into the dress he'd practically torn off her the night before. This wasn't the way she thought she'd feel after making love with a man for the first time. She'd expected to be held, comforted, reassured. But then, she'd expected that man to be her lawful husband.

She shot a look at Max, finally understanding the situation. He'd had his way with her, gotten what he'd been after since the beginning, and now he had no use for her. What was that saying about the milk and the cow? Now, as far as Max Barrett was concerned, Samantha James was all dried up.

Tears burned her eyes as she rolled up the blankets in their bedroll. Would she never learn from her mistakes with men?

They spent the day picking through the underbrush. Max would ride ahead and circle around, to make sure no one had followed them. He held his rifle, loaded and ready, across the saddle in front of him, and he'd instructed Samantha to turn tail and run if anything out of the ordinary happened. He hadn't mentioned a word about their night together, and every time he gave her that detached look, she wanted to lunge at him.

Around sunset the echo of a shotgun stopped Samantha cold. She glanced behind her, looking for Max, but he was in the midst of one of his circles and hadn't appeared behind her yet. Suddenly he came charging through the trees—on foot.

"Get down!"

He pulled her off her horse, which went charging into the forest, and they both rolled into the underbrush.

Samantha could barely breathe with him stretched out over the top of her. She spat the dirt and grass from her mouth. "What—"

He clamped his hand over her mouth and pointed through the dense foliage. Two huge men rode into view. They reminded her of the man who had attacked her by the Salmon River. They were dirty and unkempt, with straggly red hair and thick orange beards. So these were the men who were after Max. These were the men who wanted to kill him even now, as he lay protecting her with his own body.

"Barrett won't get far," one of them said.

"Not without his horse." The other snickered.

They rode past, taking their stench with them,

and the heavy chest pressing against Samantha's back finally relaxed. "I've gotta get you out of here," he said in a low voice.

She looked back over her shoulder at him and saw that he had drawn his gun. "Go after them. I'll be all right."

He shook his head, still watching as the Stricklands rode out of view. "I can't take the chance of one of them circling back for you."

She stared into his face, at the brightness of his keen blue eyes, and Samantha was struck by how much he was willing to risk in order to protect her. His job, his very being, demanded that he take the offensive, that he come out firing, but his obligation to her held him back, kept him from taking any unnecessary chances.

"Thank you," she whispered.

He looked down at her, and the indifference she'd seen in his eyes all day was gone. His mouth hovered over hers, and she closed her eyes, waiting for his kiss.

It never came.

"What say we find your horse."

She opened her eyes and blinked in surprise. "What happened to yours?"

He climbed to his feet and helped her to stand beside him. "They shot him out from under me."

"You could have been killed!"

"Shhh. If they'd wanted me dead, I'd be dead. They're crack shots, Samantha. They hit what they aim at."

Discover a World of Timeless Romance Without Leaving Home

Get 4 FREE Historical Romances from Harper Monogram.

JOIN THE TIMELESS ROMANCE READER SERVICE AND GET FOUR OF TODAY'S MOST EXCITING HISTORICAL ROMANCES FREE, WITHOUT OBLIGATION!

Imagine getting today's very best historical romances sent directly to your home — at a total savings of at least $2.00 a month. Now you can be among the first to be swept away by the latest from Candace Camp, Constance O'Banyon, Patricia Hagan, Parris Afton Bonds or Susan Wiggs. You get all that — and that's just the beginning.

PREVIEW AT HOME WITHOUT OBLIGATION AND SAVE.

Each month, you'll receive four new romances to preview without obligation for 10 days. You'll pay the low subscriber price of just $4.00 per title — a total savings of at least $2.00 a month!

Postage and handling is absolutely free and there is no minimum number of books you must buy. You may cancel your subscription at any time with no obligation.

GET YOUR FOUR FREE BOOKS TODAY ($20.49 VALUE)

FILL IN THE ORDER FORM BELOW NOW!

YES! *I want to join the Timeless Romance Reader Service. Please send me my 4 FREE HarperMonogram historical romances. Then each month send me 4 new historical romances to preview without obligation for 10 days. I'll pay the low subscription price of $4.00 for every book I choose to keep – a total savings of at least $2.00 each month – and home delivery is free! I understand that I may return any title within 10 days without obligation and I may cancel this subscription at any time without obligation. There is no minimum number of books to purchase.*

NAME_____

ADDRESS _____

CITY_____STATE_____ZIP_____

TELEPHONE_____

SIGNATURE _____

(If under 18 parent or guardian must sign. Program, price, terms, and conditions subject to cancellation and change. Orders subject to acceptance by HarperMonogram.)

GET 4 FREE BOOKS
(A $20.49 VALUE)

TIMELESS ROMANCE READER SERVICE

120 Brighton Road
P.O. Box 5069
Clifton, NJ 07015-5069

AFFIX STAMP HERE

"But why your horse?"

"Because the Stricklands like to play with their food before they eat it."

It took them half an hour, but they finally found her mare. Max retrieved his saddlebags from his dead mount, and they rode double until the moon was high in the sky and Samantha couldn't keep her eyes open for another second.

"We'll have to stop for the night," Max said. "With both of us on her she's bound to lose her footing in the dark, and we can't afford to lose another horse."

He dismounted, and Samantha fell into his arms, she was so tired. He held her against his chest, taking her full weight against him. "Are you awake?"

"No," she murmured, snuggling close to his warmth.

His laugh was soft and lulling. "For a woman on the run, you sure are calm, Miss James."

"You'll protect me, Max."

With her ear pressed to his chest, she thought she could hear his heartbeat quicken for the briefest of moments. He reached to retrieve the one bedroll from the back of her saddle and then scooped her up into his arms. Then he carried her toward a large clump of soft grass beside a tall cottonwood tree and sat down with her. Leaning back, he stretched her out on his lap.

He covered them both with the blankets. She toyed with the buttons on the front of his shirt, feeling groggy and pleasantly warm. "You made love to me last night, you know?"

He sighed and ran his hand over her hair. "I know."

"I thought you'd forgotten."

He laughed. She liked the deep, hollow sound as she rested her ear against his chest. "No, I didn't forget."

"But you wanted to." She yawned. "I know because you haven't said more than ten words to me all day."

His hand was roaming down her back, and she curved into him, liking the hard feel of him against her body. "I didn't forget, Samantha. I could never forget."

She tilted her head to look up at him, and he lifted her higher against him until they were face to face.

"I don't regret what we did last night, Max. And I wish . . ."

"You wish?"

"I wish we could . . . always be together like that."

A low moan came from the back of his throat, and he brought her mouth to his.

She melted into his warmth, withholding nothing when his tongue probed her mouth. She raised her hands to cup his face, to smooth the edges of his silky moustache, as their kiss deepened.

His hand moved between them. She felt the warmth of his fingers touch her intimately, and a shock of breath flew from her lungs. Cupping her bottom, he pressed her to his hand, and her passion exploded.

He freed himself and, moving aside the split in her bloomers, brought her down upon him. She cried out softly at their joining, so great was the heat as he moved her over him, coaxing her until she thought she might die from the pleasure.

Taking hold of his shoulders, she quickened their motions. He whispered in her ear and nibbled at her skin, moaning when she broke free of herself and fell against him in depletion. Then he rocked against her, bringing himself deep inside her, finally finding his own sweet release.

They lay together, not moving for the longest time, connected not only physically but emotionally as well. She had finally, truthfully, come to the full understanding of devotion. And she knew, that no matter what, she would love Max Barrett until the day she died.

18

With a final, hesitant glance at Max, Samantha knocked on the wooden door. They'd made a few inquiries, and the people of Logan had directed them to this well-built blue house with white trim at the edge of town. This was where they would find her aunt, Ida Olsen.

The door opened, and a large woman with orange hair stepped out onto the porch. Her skin was pale, with a faint smattering of freckles across her cheeks and the bridge of her large nose. "Sammy? Little Sammy! You're early, and, my God, girl, look at ya! You're all growed up!"

Samantha grinned as the woman clutched her and squeezed the wind out of her. "You look just like your mama, God rest her soul. Who's that ya got over there with ya?" Ida's eyes narrowed as

Max dismounted and came forward.

"This is Marshal Max Barrett. He brought me here, safe and sound."

"That remains to be seen, honey. Thank you for deliverin' my niece to me, Marshal Barrett. We'll be seein' ya, I'm sure." Then she turned and motioned Samantha into the house.

"Aunt Ida," Samantha whispered. "Max has been on the trail for almost two weeks. Don't you think you should offer him a place to rest up for a few days?"

Ida raised her red eyebrows. "Max, is it?"

Samantha forced herself not to blush and nodded.

"I suppose you're welcome to stay for a few days, Marshal Max. But the last thing I'm gonna allow is you sniffing around my niece like a wild dog. Do I make myself understood?"

Samantha's mouth dropped open. "Aunt Ida!" She glanced at Max, who appeared to be unaffected by her aunt's remarks.

"I'd be grateful for the rest. And Samantha has grown dear to me over the past couple of weeks. I'd like to see her all settled in before I go."

"Dear to ya, eh? Don't suppose you'd care to elaborate on that?"

Samantha held her breath, but Max fixed her aunt with a stoic glare and kept his jaw clamped shut.

"Didn't think so," Ida continued. "You can sleep in the barn."

* * *

Samantha carried the plate of fresh oatmeal cookies across the yard toward the barn. She pushed the creaky door open a crack and slipped inside. She paused in the doorway. Max had taken off his shirt and was working on cleaning an area for himself amid the hay, debris, and animal droppings.

"I brought you a peace offering."

He looked up at her, saw the cookies, and broke into a smile. "I could smell the cinnamon clear out here."

She handed him a cookie, and he wolfed it down in one bite.

"I'm sorry about Ida. She was always protective of my mother, and I suppose now it's my turn."

"Protective? That woman hates me."

"I don't know if it will make you feel any better, but she'd hate you even if she didn't know you."

"Yeah, Samantha, that makes me feel a hell of a lot better," he said, laughing.

"She hates lawmen. Daddy spent a lot of time away from home when he was with the marshals, and Ida swears my mom died of loneliness and worry, not consumption."

"Am I to understand your aunt does not like your father solely because he was a marshal?"

"They sit and growl at each other like two rival bears when they get together."

He reached for another cookie. "Well, at least I'm in good company."

She smiled as he turned back to making his bed. "I'm sorry you have to sleep out here."

"It's better than the wide open ground."

"Will you . . . will you stay in Logan long?"

He looked back at her, and she felt her heart squeeze in her chest. "Today and tomorrow."

"And then you'll be going after the Stricklands?"

He tossed the frame of an old lantern to a far corner of the barn. "That's right."

She wanted to ask him if he'd ever come back to Logan, but she couldn't find the courage. She felt tears well up in her eyes. "You'll be careful, won't you?"

He paused and then stretched out his hand to brush her tears away with his thumb. He moved closer, and she reached for him, curling her fingers around the muscles of his shoulders. His mouth covered hers, and a sob came out of her throat. He kissed her until she wanted to fall in a heap at his feet and beg him not to leave her. Then he tipped back her head and kissed away the tears on her cheeks.

"Don't cry, Sam," he whispered. "It hurts me so bad when you cry."

His mouth moved to her ear, and she reveled in the feel of his silken moustache as he trailed his lips down her neck. He lifted her leg, placing it high on his hip, and she felt the hardness that proved his need for her. She wrapped her hands around his waist and pulled him further against the valley of her thighs.

Neither of them heard the barn door open, and neither of them heard the sound of boots on the dry straw as someone approached.

"I'm not sure which one of ya I should shoot," Ida burst out, "the scoundrel or the ninny!"

Max let out a groan only Samantha could hear and let her leg drop back to the ground. She stepped away from him and straightened the front of her dress, her cheeks burning with the hottest blush she'd ever felt. "Aunt Ida. We—"

"Are you actually gonna try and explain this away, Sammy?"

"We were dancing."

Samantha gave Max a shocked look.

"And what dance, Marshal, requires a woman to climb a man while he's giving her a lift up with his lips?" Ida demanded.

"A very personal dance," he replied. "One that shouldn't be cut in on by unwelcome visitors."

Ida plopped her hands down onto her hips. "I told you there wouldn't be none of this going on in my house, fella."

"We are not in your house."

"You're under my roof, just the same. I won't have you two scarin' my cows dry!"

"If you're what greets them every morning, I'm surprised they're not giving jerky by now."

"Max—"

"Mister, I want you packed up and moved out before supper!"

Samantha tried again to intervene. "No—"

"It'll be my pleasure, ma'am."

"Wait!" Samantha shouted as Max stomped over to the mare. "Aunt Ida, you can't throw him out! He—he saved my life—on more than one occasion! You owe him at least two good nights of rest."

Max was already throwing things into his saddlebags. Samantha turned to her aunt, tears in her eyes, and whispered, "Please."

Ida grunted. She looked over at Max and then back at Samantha. "Two nights! And I want your word that you won't touch my niece, lawman."

Samantha held her breath, awaiting his response. "I won't give my word again," he said.

"Then I guess that settles it," Ida snapped. "*Adios.*"

"Wait!" Samantha yelled again. "I give my word. I won't come within an arm's length of Mr. Barrett, Aunt Ida. I swear. Let him stay. He needs to rest."

Ida glared at Max, and Max glared back at her. Samantha stood in between the two, glad that looks couldn't kill, because otherwise she would have been caught in the crossfire.

"Sounds reasonable to me," Ida said.

Max gave a curt nod and left the barn.

Samantha leaned against a stall in relief. "Now I

know how Mother must have felt being caught in between you and Daddy."

"There was a big difference there, Sammy. Your daddy loved your mother. He proved it by marryin' her *before* he took her to his bed."

Samantha felt her pride come up and lodge somewhere between her chest and her throat.

"Ed and I have never seen eye to eye on a lot of things, but he'd pretty near explode like a lit stick of dynamite if he knew what was goin' on between you and that lawman."

Ida shook her head and walked toward the barn door.

"I know you've made some mistakes with men before, Sammy, but this one's a doozy."

19

Max opened the screen door and stuck his nose in the kitchen. The last thing he needed this morning was to run into that red-headed heifer, Ida Olsen.

Behind him the rooster crowed loudly for the fifth time since he'd approached the house. "Once more, you long-necked fowl from hell, and you're supper," he said.

He was in a bitch of a mood. Instead of sleeping comfortably in Samantha's arms, as he had every night for the past week, he'd been forced to lie in the stench-filled hay of a damp, cold barn. He'd probably never get the smell of manure out of his clothes.

And damn if he was going to let some two-ton battle-ax get in the way of something he wanted. And he wanted Samantha James. He'd lain in his blankets on fire for her last night, burning with need like he'd never burned before. And this morning he aimed to have her.

He glanced around the kitchen, and, after seeing that no one was around, he shut the screen door and moved silently across the wooden floor, smiling to himself. There was no doubt about it. His plan was going to work.

A long while later, Samantha walked into the kitchen to the tangy smell of bacon frying. "Good morning, Aunt Ida."

"Sammy. How'd ya sleep?"

Samantha picked at the fluffy warm hotcakes on the counter. "Very soundly, actually. Has Max come in yet?"

"Didn't know he planned to."

"You are going to feed him, aren't you?"

"The man didn't show up for dinner, I figured he'd hoofed it out like I invited him to in the first place."

"He was down at the creek, bathing."

Ida turned and gave her a suspicious scowl. "And how would you know that?"

"Because when I took him a supper plate, I saw him moving in that direction with a towel in his hand."

After giving her aunt a smug smile, Samantha sat

down at the table and ate her breakfast. She was anxious to go out to the barn and see Max. Arm's length certainly didn't mean she couldn't talk to him.

Ida sat down next to her. "Been meanin' to tell ya, there's this new man in town. A nice young fella that runs the mercantile. I thought I might have him over for supper tonight. How does that sound?"

Samantha was barely listening. "Sounds fine."

"I think you're gonna like Pete, Sammy. He's a real looker. Clean, well dressed, no facial hair to speak of."

Now Samantha was paying attention. "If he's so wonderful, maybe you'd like to have supper with him alone?"

Ida scowled and dropped her fork on her plate. "He ain't for me, Sammy, he's for you. You're a beautiful girl. One look at you and Pete's gonna fall off his chair."

"Then maybe he shouldn't sit down."

Her aunt sighed and rolled her eyes. "You're gettin' the temperament of that marshal. Snippy and stubbornheaded." She pushed back from the table. "I've got animals to feed. If you could get these dishes for me I'd be grateful."

Samantha looked around the messy kitchen and somehow hid her disappointment. As she watched her aunt walk out the screen door she couldn't help but wonder if this was Ida's way of keeping her busy so she wouldn't be able to spend any time with Max.

Maybe she should head out to the barn just to make sure the two of them didn't kill each other. Then she thought better of it. Any more interference on her part, and Max was bound to start resenting it.

She carried the dirty plates and cups from the table to the sink and then crossed the room to the closet for a dishtowel. When she opened the closet door a large hand slid over her mouth, stifling her subsequent scream. Myriad terrifying scenarios flipped through her mind, but despite her fiercest struggles, she was yanked into the dark closet and the door was slammed behind her.

A familiar mouth closed over hers. Sighing with relief, she slid her hands over Max's strong shoulders and up into his hair. "What are you doing in here?" she whispered between his kisses. "You scared me half to death."

"If you don't know what I'm doing, Miss James, then we haven't spent near enough time together." His kisses seared down her neck, over her shoulders, and right through the bodice of her new yellow dress.

She fell back into his arms.

"Did your watchdog sleep at your feet last night?" he whispered against the sensitive skin of her neck.

"Ida means well."

He pulled back to look her in the eye. "What she means is to see an end to me, sweetheart. And if this Pete fellow touches you I'll break his arms."

He pulled her to him and kissed her again. She felt his hands go under her skirt and lift the material to her thighs, to her hips. He moved his hands underneath her camisole and ran his palms up and down her bare back. He planned to make love to her again, and he was making it abundantly clear.

I know you've made some mistakes with men before, Sammy, but this one's a doozy.

Samantha pulled away from him. "We can't do this."

Max's hands continued to stroke and tempt her weakening flesh. "Why not? The gigantic paragon of womanly virtues is out feedin' the chickens." He cupped her bottom with one hand and lifted her against his hard body.

She pressed her hands against his chest. "I . . . I gave my word."

He pulled her arms down from around his neck and held them to her sides. "There. Now, I'm not within your arm's length." He pressed her back against the closet wall and began working on the knot of her bloomers.

"No, Max, we can't!"

Her angry voice finally got through to him, and he backed up against the other wall. He ran his hands through his hair. "I want you so bad I can taste you. Even when you're standing a foot away."

"But Ida—"

"No 'but Ida!'" he growled. "I swear to God I'm gonna shoot that woman."

"She's only looking out for my best interests."

"Are you saying that I'm not in your best interests?"

"Well, I don't know. I'm standing here in a dark closet with you and you're mad that I won't . . . that I won't—"

"Do what you've done with me twice before?"

She felt her face heat up. "I may have done this with you twice before, Mr. Barrett, but that doesn't mean I'm condemned to do it for the rest of my life!"

"Condemned?"

"As a matter of fact, if I choose to never let you touch me again, that is my prerogative!"

He leaned forward and stared deeply into her eyes. "I'll be leaving tomorrow at first light, Samantha. Either you come to me before then, or I'll be comin' to you."

His declaration scared the wits out of her, and Samantha scampered out of the closet. Breathing hard, she leaned back against the closed door, and there stood her aunt, looking more suspicious than ever.

"Don't suppose you saw a rat in there by the name of Barrett?"

"I—I was just looking for some dishsoap."

"'Course you were. I never thought for a second you were going back on your word."

Samantha smiled weakly, and to her horror felt the closet door begin to open. She pressed back against it with all her might, but in the end Max's determination to get out proved too much for her meager weight.

Ida scowled at the marshal. "I suppose you were just lookin' for dishsoap too?"

Max gave her a tired look and headed out the kitchen door, muttering, "Whatever I was looking for, I sure the hell didn't find it."

Samantha stood at the front of the tiny schoolhouse, staring at the benches where her students would sit, and at the chalkboard where they would learn their sums. It was Friday, April 15th. School wasn't scheduled to begin again until Monday, but she'd wanted to see the building, and she'd wanted to find something to do to take her mind off Max Barrett.

The previous teacher, Mrs. Strithright, had left the primers on the teacher's desk, along with a note explaining where the students were in their studies and which students needed particular attention. Jonathon Cobble was the troublemaker according to the note. *Best to get him in the corner first thing each morning to keep the others from being too distracted.* Samantha wondered if Max had ever been branded a troublemaker.

She pulled the chair out from under the desk and sat down, wishing she had just one answer to the questions roaming around in her head. Would Max ever come back her? Did he love her? Was she making a big mistake in letting herself love him?

She supposed the answer to the last question made little difference, seeing how she'd hardly had a say in the matter. Love had just sort of snuck up on her when she hadn't been looking.

The front door opened, and she jumped in surprise.

"Hello," a man called. The sun framed a tall figure in the doorway, and Samantha shielded her eyes to see better.

"Hello," she called back.

The man moved forward, a smile playing on his thin lips. He stopped in front of her and took his hat off, revealing a mop of dark hair. "The name's Stanley. Sheriff Stanley, ma'am. I suppose you're the new teacher?"

Samantha stood and held out her hand. "That's right, Sheriff. It's a pleasure to meet you."

He held onto her hand a moment longer than necessary, and Samantha felt apprehension slip up her spine until he finally let it loose.

"The pleasure is all mine, ma'am. I saw the door cracked open there, and thought I'd check to be sure there weren't no kids messing with the teachin' things."

Samantha looked up and noticed he'd shut the door behind him. They were alone in the secluded room. She came around the desk, walked toward the nearest window, and pushed up the sash. A breeze of fresh mountain air lifted the hair from her face. She turned back to the man and smiled again, not sure why his presence made her so uncomfortable.

"Everything is fine here, Sheriff. I'll be sure to lock up tight before I leave."

He moved closer to her, and she realized what it was about him that made her so nervous. It was his eyes. They were gold—no, almost yellow—like the eyes of the man who'd attacked her by the river. She glanced at his dark hair and reminded herself that this poor unsuspecting man was not a Strickland.

"My office is just down the street if you need anything, ma'am. Anything at all." He put his hat back on, tugged on the brim, and left.

Samantha sat back down at the desk and wiped at the sweat that had trickled down her neck. She needed to force that scene by the river out of her mind. She certainly couldn't go through her life terrified of every golden-eyed man she met. Taking a deep breath, she cracked open one of the readers and began preparing her Monday lessons.

Pete Holden couldn't believe his rotten luck.

He was sitting next to the prettiest young lady he'd ever seen, but in Ida Olsen's house, and with a lawman who looked fit to kill—him!

His eyes continued to stray to the marshal, who was standing rigidly in the kitchen doorway.

"You should take Samantha for a ride in that new-fangled buggy ya just bought, Pete," Ida said, ending a particularly tense moment of silence. "I bet she'd get a kick outta that."

Pete glanced uneasily at the man in the doorway, thinking he'd probably get a kick out of it too!

"How's tomorrow for ya?" Ida went on.

"I'm sure that's much too short a notice for Mr. Holden, Aunt Ida. Perhaps he has other things planned for tomorrow," Samantha said.

"Nonsense. You've got time to take my niece on a little buggy ride, don't ya Pete?"

Pete Holden recognized an order when he heard one. Looking back and forth between the marshal and the aunt, he debated as to which one was worse. He doubted Max Barrett would do more to him than bloody his nose, being a lawman. But Ida Olsen would surely sit on Pete and squash his intestines if he didn't do what she was prodding him to do. And he'd probably have to live in the same town as her for the better part of his life.

All this, coupled with the fact that Samantha James was a very attractive young woman, made Pete's decision rather easy.

He turned his back on the marshal's icy blue stare. "I'd be honored if you would accompany me on a ride tomorrow, Miss James. It is a rather nice buggy, if you'll pardon my boasting."

Samantha's smile came across as a bit weak, in Pete's point of view, but she said, "All right, Mr. Holden. I suppose—"

Pete jumped at the sound of the kitchen screen slamming shut. The marshal had, apparently, needed some air.

Max paused in the hallway of the darkened house later that night, his muscles tense. Every shadow resembled that of an enraged bull elephant by the name of Ida Olsen. He only wanted to look at Samantha one more time in her sleep. One more time before he left the next day.

He quietly opened Samantha's door and slipped into her room. In her sleep she'd kicked her blankets to the foot of the bed. She'd apparently drifted off before blowing out her lantern, and it cast shadows over her thinly gowned body.

He crossed the room and lowered himself down beside her on the bed, brushing the hair from her face.

She opened her eyes. Smiling, still half asleep, she curled up tighter to her pillow. "Couldn't sleep?"

"I guess I need to hear your snores."

Her eyes cleared, and she frowned. "You're not here to—to . . ."

Max's temper flared. The thought had crossed his mind, and she seemed pretty damn upset at the idea. "What's the matter, Miss James? Your new fella

Pete Holden wouldn't like it if another man's hands were on you the night before your buggy ride?"

She sat up in bed. "Pete Holden is not my *new fella*. And I don't appreciate your tone."

"Well, I don't appreciate you accepting that pinched-faced weasel's invitation!"

"Keep your voice down. I don't give a flying fig what you think!" she rasped back. "The invitation was politely offered, and you've certainly got no claim on me!"

He took her by the arm and pulled her toward his face. "The night you appeased my rabid lusts I laid claim to you, Miss James, and you'd be best served not to forget that."

She tried to shake off his hand, but he only tightened his grip. He felt like he was losing her, and the idea was killing him. Finally, he let go of her arm. "Take off your nightgown."

"What?"

"I plan to have a going-away present, Miss James, and you're it."

Tears pooled on her lashes. "Bastard," she whispered. "I won't be a toy for you or anyone else. If you need appeasement, go find yourself a whore!"

Max sat back and pressed his palms against his eyes. This whole thing was turning out all wrong. "A whore won't do," he said quietly.

"Your tender sentiments mean the world to me. Get out of my room. Out!"

He paused, torn between storming out of the room,

the house, her life, and burrowing into bed with her. She'd been his reason to wake up every morning for the past two weeks, and he didn't think he knew how to move forward without her. Suddenly, he was afraid.

He stood up and went to the door. "Good-bye, Max," he heard her choke out before he closed the door behind him.

He felt tears burning his eyes as he made his way through the house. He hadn't yet reached the kitchen door when something swooped down and smacked him across the face. With a loud curse, he pivoted around and came face to face with Ida Olsen and her broom.

"If you think for one second I'm gonna let you break that girl's heart then you're dumber than I thought," she said, emphasizing her words with another blow of her broom.

"Lady, if you hit me with that thing one more time, you're gonna find it sticking out from your ears."

"Don't you threaten me, *Mister Marshal*. I've lived long enough to learn how to deal with the likes of you."

He took a step toward the woman. "You know, I've had just about enough of you scoffing at my profession. I earned my badge, lady, and I'm damn proud to wear it."

"Well, congratulations," she said. "But your overstated pride won't do a whole hell of a lot of good for Samantha. How do you think she's gonna feel when you leave? She won't know from one minute to the next if you're layin' dead somewhere, the wolves and coyotes pickin' at your bones."

"I'm sure you'll see that Pete Holden comforts her regularly."

"You can bet I'll do whatever I think is best for my niece."

"Tell me something, lady, what if I were best for Samantha? Me, a lawman."

"That would never happen, Barrett. Lawmen don't understand the word commitment. They're too busy tryin' to catch themselves the big one, make themselves a hero. They run off and don't give a second thought to the families they leave behind to worry."

Max thought of his family in Carson, which he hardly ever saw, and Ida's words stung him like a bad snakebite. She was right. He was no good for Samantha. The best thing he could do for her was get the hell out of her life and let her move on with someone reliable like Pete Holden.

"I'll be leaving at first light—"

"Tomorrow? You're leavin' Sammy on her birthday? Lord, ain't that just like a lawman."

Max blinked. Tomorrow was Samantha's birthday? A vision came to him of Pete Holden feeding Samantha cake and telling her to forget all about that snake-in-the-grass lawman who'd left her on her birthday.

"Like I said, I'll be leaving at first light . . . the day after tomorrow." He gave Ida a broad smile, which appeared to startle her, and then left the house.

20

Samantha sat beside Pete in a meadow outside of town. Pete was admiring the magnificent view of the Rockies, and she was rubbing her nose, fighting her allergic reaction to the wild flowers surrounding them. When he looked back at her she managed a weak smile. Her legs were beginning to itch from the fragrant flowers beneath her.

"Maybe we should sit in the buggy," she said, trying to keep a plea from her voice.

"Nonsense," Pete replied. "It's a lovely morning for basking in the sunshine."

Samantha cringed as he began to weave a wreath for her to wear around her neck.

"How long have you and the marshal known each other?"

She was startled by his question. The last person

she wanted to talk about was Max Barrett. He'd ridden out that morning, and she'd probably never see him again. The idea made her chest tighten. "Only a month or so."

"Then it's a strange situation, you traveling alone with him through the wilderness."

She could tell by his curious eyes that he wanted to hear the whole sordid mess, bit by bit. "It's a long story, really, Mr. Holden. I doubt you'd be very interested in it at all."

He touched her hand. "Please. Call me Pete. And I'd be very interested in anything you had to say."

"Really, Mr. Holden, I don't think—"

"A beautiful young woman like you has no need to think, Samantha. Your very existence is enough."

Samantha didn't know whether to be insulted or flattered. Somehow she managed to hold back a laugh.

"Samantha, I'm so happy you agreed to this outing. I think it's going to be quite wonderful having you in town. I've only been here a week or so myself, so we could make friends together."

Samantha's conscience was pricked. The young man was staring at her with such tender eyes. She shouldn't be here with him. Her heart had long since been lost, for better or for worse, and there was no hope of getting it back.

"Your aunt tells me the marshal's leaving tomorrow."

Her head snapped up. "Tomorrow? I was under the impression that he'd already left."

"Apparently he decided to stay on for your birthday."

Samantha warmed at the thought and couldn't help the faint smile that touched her lips.

"You do of course know the man is helplessly in love with you, Miss James." Pete looked intently into her eyes. "Might I ask if you are helplessly in love with him?"

"I'm certainly not helpless."

"Are you denying you love him?"

"I'm denying he loves me. His affection toward me is purely in the . . . in the physical sense."

Pete patted her hand. "There are men and then there are scoundrels, Samantha. Sometimes it's hard for an innocent young lady such as yourself to tell the difference."

Her history with men had certainly proven that. Only now she wasn't so innocent. "I think we should go." She stood up and walked to the buggy.

Pete followed behind her, a look of pained sympathy on his face. "He'll be gone tomorrow, Samantha. Then you and I can start fresh."

She accepted Pete's help onto the buggy. She was surprised that Max hadn't left yet, but she knew it made little difference. He would be leaving tomorrow, and taking her heart and soul with him.

* * *

In the early afternoon Max rode Samantha's mare down the main street of Logan. The town was quaint and well kept. Buildings were painted in sedate colors with an artist's perfection, signs were hung neatly, even the streets were clean, free of the stench and manure that plagued most cities.

He reined up in front of the sheriff's office, his boots thudding loudly on the boardwalk as he approached and pushed open the door.

The place smelled of sweat and vomit, the latter a present, no doubt, from the local town drunk. Even a fine upstanding city like Logan had its share of problems, he supposed.

A dark-haired man sitting behind a large oak desk looked up at him with deep-set, almost yellow eyes. "Can I help you?"

Max eyed the man. His hair was tousled, his face looked almost too youthful to shave, and he had, of all things, a sweet-pop pursed between his lips. The fellow was just the kind of sheriff a tame city like Logan would hire. The kind of man who wasn't quite sure how to cock his pistol or even get it clear of his holster.

Max tossed his badge on the desk, and the young sheriff's eyes widened. "U.S. Marshal Barrett." If it was possible, the fellow's eyes rounded even more. "I want your help with something."

"Barrett?"

"And you are?"

"Stanley." The sheriff rose from his seat and

stuck out his hand. "Guy Stanley. And might I say that it's a mighty fine pleasure to meet you, Marshal Barrett. What exactly can I do for ya?"

Max sat himself down on the edge of the man's desk. "There's a woman in town I want you to keep an eye on for me."

Stanley looked interested—a little too interested as far as Max was concerned.

"Is she a pretty little thing with big brown eyes and dark brown hair?"

Max nodded.

"About this tall?"—Stanley held up a hand—"and finely built?"

"You seem to know her pretty well."

"A brand-new single lady is hard to keep secret in this town, Marshal. What's this sweet young teacher done that you want me to keep my eye on her?"

Max felt a heat of rage run through him. He didn't appreciate this man's interest in Samantha. "Not a thing, Sheriff. I'd just like you to watch out for her, is all." He leaned across the desk. "And if anything happens to her I'll rip your beating heart out and feed it to the rats."

The sheriff gulped. "Don't worry, Marshal, ain't nobody gonna mess with the woman as long as I'm alive."

"Good. She's staying with her Aunt Ida just outside of town."

Guy let out a pained groan. "Not that large, redheaded heathen. Lord almighty, she hates me!"

Max smiled. For once, he admired Ida's taste in men. "I'll be leaving tomorrow morning. Keep a good eye peeled for at least the next few weeks."

He snatched up his badge and left the office, figuring that with Guy's badge and Ida's broom, Samantha couldn't be in safer company. He didn't expect any real trouble anyway. There was no way in hell the Stricklands could know where Samantha was.

Max heard the sound of faint, off-key singing as he rode up to the house with his new horse in tow. He left both horses in the barn and walked toward the kitchen door, the poorly sung strains of *Happy Birthday* battering his ears.

As he pushed open the screen, his gaze settled on Samantha's smile. She was dressed in deep green, and her rich brown hair was loose around her shoulders. Before her sat a chocolate cake decorated with tiny candles all over the top.

"Haaappy birrrrthdaaay toooo youuuu," Ida finished, with Pete Holden's grating voice trailing behind by a beat. "Now blow out the candles, honey."

Samantha took a huge breath and blew out all twenty of the candles in one long puff.

"Yeah, smile now," Ida said, laughing. "Twenty more years and that feat'll be next to impossible."

Samantha looked up, and Max caught her eye.

The smile slipped from her face, making his heart tumble over in his chest. She was still hurt by the things he'd said the night before.

"Would you like a piece of cake?" Her question drew Ida and Pete's attention, and they both looked up at him.

"I'd love one."

He took the chair across the table from her and didn't notice when Ida slid a piece of cake beneath his nose. He was too busy looking at Samantha. She was smiling once again as she sliced into the cake, and her brown eyes were bright. He was reminded of the time those eyes had stared at his bare chest beside a campfire, at how breathless and weak their innocence had made him. The two of them had spent almost every waking hour together for the past two weeks and now he wasn't sure he remembered how to go through a day without her.

Pete was holding out a tiny black box to Samantha and fingering his gray vest nervously. "It's just something I picked up for you. A spur of the moment gift when your aunt informed me last night that today was your birthday."

Max closed his eyes, feeling as if a hard fist had just slammed him in the stomach. He hadn't thought to get her a present.

Samantha gave Holden a warm smile, one that Max felt all the way to his trigger finger. "This is very thoughtful of you, Mr. Holden. Thank you."

She worked the tiny latch at the side of the box

and popped it open. Nestled in a bed of silk lay a tiny silver neckchain.

Max shot the man a glare. No man gave a lady something so extravagant unless there were strings attached. He was about to say this out loud when Samantha spoke up.

"Mr. Holden, I can't accept this."

Max was relieved for a moment, and then he wanted to strangle Ida Olsen when she said, "Of course you can, honey, it's a birthday gift. Perfectly acceptable."

Pete shuffled. "It's only a small token of my esteem." His eyes meet Max's. "My friendlike esteem."

Samantha hesitated, then drew the chain around her neck. Max felt her slip a little further away from him. He did feel a little better when Pete poked into his pocket, yanked out some badly damaged wild flowers, and handed them to her. Not only did the things look like they'd been handed down from generation to generation, but Samantha was extremely allergic, and the fellow obviously didn't realize it.

"That was a very kind thought, Mr. Holden," Ida said. But she was eyeing Max. "An almost total stranger rememberin' to buy my niece a present. What a kind young man you are."

Max took the jab with more ease than he felt, although in his mind he was hefting Ida up with some sturdy rope and pulleys and dropping her in the pig trough.

"I don't suppose you'll be courtin' my niece come tomorra', Mr. Holden?" Ida went on. She was continuing to look over at Max too many times for it to go unnoticed by the others in the room.

Pete stammered for an answer, and Max rose from his chair. If he didn't leave the house he was going to kill Samantha's aunt with his bare hands. "I've got some things to take care of before I leave tomorrow," he announced. He turned to Samantha. "Happy birthday, Miss James."

Once in the barn, he tore the saddle from Samantha's horse and began packing his saddlebags. He was going to keep himself busy and not think of her living out her life with that weasel, Pete Holden. But his lips tightened with the effort, and his mind wandered despite his resolve.

He threw the saddlebags against the wall.

A clutter of objects fell to the floor, his many possessions from years of travel. He walked over to the heap, determined to try again to pack the bags with some semblance of calm, but a flicker of gold caught his eye. He crouched down, and a smile turned up the ends of his moustache. There among the jerky sticks and old bullets lay just the gift he needed.

After quelling her smiling aunt with a hot glare, Samantha followed Max to the barn. She found him bent over the ground, staring at something in his hand. "Max?"

He looked up, and her heart practically shattered in her chest. How could she love him so much and he love her so little? "Finish your cake already?" he asked.

She shrugged. "Would you like me to go get yours?"

"Nah." He turned back to his packing.

She looked around her at the mess on the floor. Cans of beans, strips of jerky, old hanks of cloth, dirty pieces of twine, and even some bullets lay scattered all around him. "Cleaning house?"

"Just sorting through a few things."

Sorting through? It looked like he'd tossed his saddlebags in the air just to see what might fall out. "Pete tells me you're leaving tomorrow at first light."

"Pete?"

"He found out from Ida."

Max grunted. "So, how was your buggy ride?"

"I thought you were leaving this morning."

"Did Holden take you to a scenic spot?"

"I'd thought you'd left without saying good-bye."

"Did he make you wreaths out of wild flowers and stare longingly into your eyes?"

"Can you forget about Pete for a minute!"

"Can you?"

Samantha paused. "Pete Holden doesn't have anything to do with us."

Max laughed, and the sound rumbled through the barn. "Pete Holden has everything to do with us, Samantha. For one thing, I'm leaving and he's staying."

"Pete's just a friend—"

"Oh, he wants to be a whole lot more than that."

"He can want until the cows come home, I'm in . . . I'm in*capable* of becoming involved at the moment." Dear Lord, she'd almost blurted that she was in love with him. That really would have made a mess of things.

He moved closer to her. "Pete can give you everything you need, Samantha. A home, a family—"

"Since when are you such an expert on what I need?"

He looked into her eyes. "All right, then you tell me, tell me what you need."

"Respect . . . and . . . and"—she trailed off as he kissed her once, twice, three times—"and understanding . . . and . . ."

"And passion. Don't forget passion, Samantha," he murmured against her mouth.

She slid her hands over his shoulders. "Yes. . . . Passion."

He settled his mouth over hers, and her legs felt weak. She locked her fingers around his neck as he lifted her off the ground and kissed her as she'd never been kissed before.

"I'm sorry I acted like such an ass last night," he said.

She smiled at the warmth in his eyes.

"And I do have a present for you."

He set her down on her feet and reached into his pocket.

Samantha shook her head. "I don't need a gift from you—"

He opened up his hand, and she stared down at an incredibly delicate golden brooch of two entwined hearts. "Oh, it's beautiful!"

"It's an antique. It belonged to my grandmother, and I want you to have it."

"I don't know . . ."

"You'll take Holden's gift but you won't take mine?"

"But Mr. Holden's gift was a simple chain, one he probably chose from his mercantile before he left for the party. This is . . . this is an heirloom. It must hold a great deal of meaning for you and your family."

He took the brooch from her palm and pinned it to the bodice of her dress. "I want you to have it."

She looked into his eyes and soon found herself lost.

One look from those eyes and a woman would jump to do his bidding.

"Thank you," she whispered.

She wanted to be back in his arms, to hold onto him so tightly that he would change his mind and stay. But she realized the folly in that as soon as he stepped away from her. Max Barrett was a man who wouldn't be tied down. He was leaving in the morning, and nothing she could do or say was going to stop him.

21

Samantha walked barefoot across the cold floorboards down the darkened hallway to the back of the house. She paused just outside Ida's door and listened closely for the woman's snores. Then she walked past the sitting room, through the kitchen, and out the back door.

Her nerves grew jumpy as she picked her way carefully across the rocky ground toward the barn. Why in the world hadn't she thought to put on her shoes?

She took a deep breath, nudged open the barn door, and stole a peek inside. Max appeared to be sleeping, lying wrapped in a blanket on a pile of hay.

She crept toward him, mindful of the sharp pieces of dry straw lying on the dirt floor. Finally standing next to him, she swallowed hard, her conscience screaming for her to run back to the house and not look back.

His eyes were closed, and his face looked so peaceful she thought she might cry. She reached down to him but pulled up short, knowing that touching him would only wake him up, and she wasn't prepared for that. She hated long good-byes, but, lying in her bed, she knew she'd never be able to live with herself if she didn't come and look at him one final time.

She stood there and memorized every line of his face, every feature. She took in his mussed hair and his smooth moustache, stared at his strong hands, and remembered the feel of them rough against her skin. "I'm going to miss you, Max Barrett," she said softly and turned on her heel for the door.

A large hand encircled her ankle, stopping her in her tracks. "Was there something you wanted to speak with me about, Miss James?"

Samantha paused and looked back at him. His hand was still gripped tightly around her ankle. "I"—she looked down at the brown wool blanket that barely covered him—"I just wanted to see if you were awake. I wasn't sleeping well, and I—"

His hand traveled up underneath the hem of her nightgown, along her calf, and, like a hot brand, crept to the hollow at the back of her knee.

She felt heat flood her cheeks, and she looked around the dimly moonlit barn, anywhere but at him, at his eyes.

He ran his hand further up her leg, to the back of her thigh, and squeezed gently, urging her toward him. "Come here," he said softly.

Unwilling and unable to resist, Samantha sank to her knees beside him, his hand still riding high beneath her nightgown.

"Tell me what you want," he whispered.

She was drowning in the liquid pool of his blue eyes. "I want to say good-bye."

"Good-bye?" He rolled to his side, causing the blanket to slip to his bare hips. His fingers caressed the tingling skin of her leg. His eyes locked with hers. "Do you want a kiss, Samantha?"

She nodded, completely captivated by the passion burning in his gaze.

"Then take one."

She gathered her courage and leaned forward, touching her mouth to his. His lips were soft, pliant, there for her bidding, and her hands rose to his hard chest. She drew closer to him and opened her mouth, running her tongue along his lips as he'd done to her so many times before. She raised her arms, pushed her fingers through his hair, and stretched herself out over him.

He quickly did away with her nightgown.

With her bare breasts against his chest, she threw herself further into the kiss. His hands pressed her against his hard body, and she felt adrift on a hot breeze. She was a budding flower, and he was the sun.

With one quick tug, he pulled the blanket out from between them.

Samantha found herself rolled beneath him, his intense blue eyes searching hers. "Have you had your kiss, madame?" he asked hoarsely.

"I couldn't . . . I couldn't let you go without seeing you one last time."

He kissed her eyes, her nose, her chin. His hands explored her body, and he tasted her lips and her skin and whispered delicious things to her. Most of all she was seduced by his soft, coaxing voice.

He slipped his hand down to that secret part of her that he alone knew, and soon Samantha was forgetting her sorrow. Soon her thoughts were crashing into focus on only the two of them, together.

She whispered his name as his fingers pushed her closer and closer to the edge. Her body tensed of its own accord, and the night burst into a million shining stars that showered down on her and danced through her mind.

Max framed her face with his hands. "I told you once that you were mine." He pushed himself inside her, and she gasped at the deep pleasure. "That will never change."

She gave herself up to him, giving him free reign over her body and her senses. They were one, the way they should be, the way God had intended.

She cherished each of his movements and each whispered endearment, until, once again, her passion began to build. Sighs of pleasure slipped from her lips as she dug her fingers into the flexing muscles of his back.

And when his release came, she cried out his name and sobbed with the knowledge that this would be their last time.

22

Samantha sat on the porch steps in the cold morning air, drinking a strong cup of coffee and staring off at the northernmost mountains around the valley. Max had left two days ago. He'd saddled his horse and ridden out before the sun had risen, before she'd even awakened from their bed of hay in the barn.

The memories of their last night together were still strong enough to warm her body when she contemplated them. She wondered if they were strong enough to last her a lifetime. They were all she had left of Max, memories and his grandmother's brooch.

She looked down and pressed the golden pin against her heart. Max would never forget her. She could believe nothing else as she tried to make it through each day.

She'd spent the last two days going through the motions of living. Putting on a smile whenever one was needed, starting her first day at school as if nothing out of the ordinary had happened to her in the past month. Ida kept telling her she was just feeling lonely, being in a new place, but Samantha knew it was much more than that.

It was as if a piece of her was missing. Every now and then she'd turn and expect to find Max standing behind her with a smile turning up the edges of his moustache. She still woke up each morning wondering why she didn't feel his warmth beside her. And she would never, never be able to look at the sky without thinking of his eyes.

Ida couldn't understand it. Pete tried to distract her, but nothing seemed to help. Nothing and no one could erase the imprint of Max Barrett on her heart.

Samantha stood up on the porch. There was a cloud of dust kicking up in the distance. A rider was coming toward the house. She shielded her eyes with her hand, daring to hope that it was Max, riding like the wind to come back for her. Her heart sank when a dark-headed rider halted in front of her and climbed off his horse.

"Good morning, Sheriff Stanley."

He looked at her for just a second too long with those yellow eyes, and Samantha's hands began to shake around her coffee mug. Then he tugged off his hat. "Marshal Barrett asked me to keep a close eye on ya. I thought I'd come by and see how things were goin'."

"That's very kind of you, Sheriff, and of Marshal Barrett."

The sheriff smiled and sat down next to her on the porch. "Any trouble so far?"

"No. Everything's been quiet. Honestly, I really don't need you to look out for me—"

"Where was it, exactly, the marshal said he was headed?"

She blinked. "I'm not sure. If he'd wanted you to know that wouldn't he have told you himself?"

The sheriff gave her a quick smile. "Well, I am only trying to help, ma'am. And I think you'd do best to cooperate." He leaned close to her. "You never know when I could come in handy—"

"What the hell are you doin' on my porch!" Ida lumbered out the screen door and smacked the sheriff with her broom. "Get the hell away from my niece and away from my house!"

Sheriff Stanley was up and off the porch in one quick motion. "Good God, you are a wretched old woman!"

"And I'm gonna make you look like the bad side of last week if you don't get your bony behind off my property!"

With a sneer at Ida and a stilted bow to Samantha, the sheriff of Logan mounted up and rode off.

Samantha stared after him. "That man gives me the creeps."

"As well he should. He's only been our sheriff for two months, and he thinks he owns the whole damn town. Blew into Logan right after a crazy bunch of hoodlums came in and picked off our previous sheriff. A good man, Sheriff Robbins was. A bit slow on the draw, poor fella, but a damn fine man."

"Sheriff Stanley wasn't a resident of Logan before?"

"Nope. He took up the badge after conning most of the townsfolk about his upright qualities." Ida's green eyes narrowed. "He didn't fool me none, though. I know me a bad seed when I see one."

A chill ran up Samantha's spine. "Max wouldn't have asked Sheriff Stanley to see to my safety if he didn't trust him."

"To hell with Barrett. Do *you* trust Stanley?"

Samantha grimaced. "My first instinct is to stay as far away from him as possible."

Ida laughed. "I knew you had Olsen blood pumping in you somewhere, honey. If Stanley's payin' you any attention, you can bet he's up to no good."

Max reined in and bent down over his horse's neck to look at the hoof prints in the dirt. He'd been tracking two horses, one with a bent nail in his shoe, for the last two days. He wondered when Zack Strickland was going to get that shoe fixed and then realized that he never would. It was all part of the game that the gang liked to play with lawmen.

They were headed for Nevada, as far as he could tell, and he was still a good day behind them. He straightened up in his saddle and continued onward, slow and easy. Traveling day and night, he'd have them before nightfall tomorrow.

Nightfall. Invariably it meant loneliness, and thoughts of Samantha. She would have started her classes by now. He wondered if the students liked her. But of course they liked her. Who wouldn't love Samantha?

He scowled at his train of thought and concentrated on the trail. He couldn't afford to be distracted during daylight hours. Nightfall would come soon. And then so would the longing.

Sheriff Stanley walked into the telegraph office and pounded the bell on the counter to catch the attention of the bald man sitting behind the teletype desk.

The man turned around and peered at him through wire spectacles. "Can I help you, Sheriff?"

"I need to send a telegram to Harriet. It's urgent law business."

"And what city is this Harriet in?"

"Harriet, Nevada, you idiot! I want it sent to a Mr. Zack Stokeman." Guy leaned on his elbows on the counter. "The message goes as follows. 'Got what ya need right here, stop. Hurry but be careful, stop.' Ya got that, Beeman?"

"I got it," Mr. Beeman said, jotting down the message on his pad of paper.

"Make sure ya send it right away. Mr. Stri—Mr. Stokeman don't like to be kept waitin'."

23

One full week after Max left, Samantha spotted a cloud of rider's dust on the horizon and held her breath once again. Maybe Max had taken care of the Stricklands and was riding back to her.

When she distinguished two riders a disappointed frown fell over her face. She wasn't expecting company, and didn't care to greet any, so she went into the house and to her bedroom, hoping they might think the house empty and ride away.

A few minutes later she heard the front door slam open. Then came sounds of furniture being shoved aside and tossed around the sitting room. Her heart began to race in fear.

"We know you're in here, lady!"

Two huge red-haired men barged into her room. Triumphant leers spread across their hairy faces.

"Miss Samantha James, I presume," the taller one said. The other laughed, showing his blackened teeth.

Samantha tried to calm down and summon the courage to look angry. She glared straight into the larger man's yellow eyes. "Get the hell out of my house!"

Her bravado earned her a boisterous laugh.

"You got spunk, I'll say that much for ya, lady." He grabbed her by the hair and pulled her up. "Too bad I don't like women with spunk!"

She cried out, and the man's eyes lit up. He obviously was enjoying her pain. She swore to herself she wouldn't make another sound.

With a sickeningly slow motion, the man ran his hand up her hip, yanking her hair harder when she squirmed. He finally settled his rough fingers on one of her breasts. "Nice," he said, leering. "Very nice." His rancid breath turned her stomach. "Tell me, has the noble marshal saddlebroke ya yet?"

His hand made a move to go between her thighs, and with a violent ram of her knee, Samantha had him doubled over.

She would have tried for the door, but the other man blocked her path. The man in front of her regained control and slapped her. She was knocked to the bed and could taste blood where her teeth had cut into her lip.

The huge man towered over her, narrowing his eyes. "You're gonna die, bitch. It'll be my pleasure to see to it."

The front door slammed open again. "Samantha?" Ida called.

"Get the sheriff!" she shouted, and another slap connected with her numbing face.

"Take care of the old woman, Tyler. We don't have time for messin' around."

Finding strength from somewhere deep within, Samantha sprang from the bed. She took the heavy brass lamp from the table next to her and raised it over her head. "Maybe I am gonna die, Mister," she said, "but I plan to take you with me."

A harsh laugh shook the man's massive shoulders. "Do you have any idea how many lawmen have threatened me, lady? Any idea how many I've killed? More than you can count! Now, you put that thing down or you won't make it through the next minute alive."

Samantha clung to her heavy weapon with both hands. "What do you want with me? I don't—don't even know you!"

The man smiled, an ugly smile that made Samantha's flesh crawl. "I'm goin' marshal huntin', sweet thing. And you're gonna be my bait."

Samantha knew now that these men had to be the infamous Stricklands. Terror for Max made her squeeze the lamp harder. "It'll never work. Max Barrett is too smart to fall for one of your tricks!"

The man's yellow eyes narrowed. "I have a

feeling where you're concerned he ain't so smart at all—Tyler! Have you got that woman taken care of yet!"

Samantha waited anxiously for Tyler Strickland's response. She hadn't heard the sound of shot being fired, but a knife could be as deadly as a gun. She closed her eyes and prayed her aunt was all right.

Strickland took a step closer, and she tensed, raising the lamp higher. "I swear I'll do it," she warned him.

He took out his gun and pointed it at her. "I guess it's all the same to me. You can die now or you can die later."

He was calling her bluff. Unfortunately she didn't have the courage to call his. She closed her eyes and lowered the object back to the table.

Strickland's hand shot out and gripped her by the hair. He dragged her down the hall, past the destroyed sitting room, and into the kitchen.

The sound of Ida's screech was music to Samantha's ears. "Get your filthy hands off my niece!" Ida was pressed against the counter. Tyler Strickland was holding a gun on her and shaking his head.

"Shut up, old woman. Why ain't you shot her yet, Tyler?"

"Z-Zack? D-do you believe in ghosts?"

"What the hell are you talkin' about?" Zack pushed Samantha into a chair and held her there.

"This old woman, Zack. She—she looks just like Ma."

"I ain't your ma, you lowdown snake!" Ida shouted. "Your ma most likely died the moment she laid eyes on ya!"

Zack Strickland gave Ida an assessing stare. "Yeah, yeah she does look like Ma. So?"

"Even has that endearin' grate to her voice, don't ya think, Zack?"

Zack Strickland seemed to be growing very impatient. "So?"

"So, I can't shoot her, Zack. It'd be like puttin' a hole through Ma."

"Oh, for—she ain't Ma! Look at her! She ain't got half the moles on her face Ma had!"

A loud knock echoed through the house, and Samantha raised hopeful eyes to the front door. "Watch 'em, Tyler."

Zack Strickland left the room, and Samantha gave her aunt a bolstering smile which left the whole left side of her face aching.

Her aunt winced. "Don't be grinning for my sake, Sammy honey. You're liable to break something, permanent."

Muffled voices were heard, and then Zack Strickland reentered the kitchen—with none other than Sheriff Guy Stanley. Samantha would have shouted with joy, but the sheriff and Mr. Strickland looked awfully friendly with each other. And then she remembered Guy Stanley's yellow eyes, and a sickness rose up in her stomach.

"We're movin' out, Tyler. Our loyal cousin here

spotted Barrett about two miles outside of town. Our marshal's gonna be here any minute."

The sheriff smiled at Samantha. "Well, howdy again, Miss James. Ya see, I told ya that being my friend might come in handy someday."

Ida let out a gasp. "Why you lyin', low-down, yellow-bellied, two-faced—"

"Why ain't you killed her yet?" Sheriff Stanley demanded.

"Tyler was just about to take care of that for us—"

Samantha sprang from her chair, rushed the unsuspecting sheriff, and grappled for his gun. But two men against one woman proved too much, and she ended up squeezed against Zack Strickland's sweaty chest.

"She's a wild one, this one is," Guy said, laughing. "You're gonna have your hands full with her. Why she'd risk her neck to save that old biddy, God only knows."

Zack's eyes settled with cruel contemplation upon Samantha. "'Cause she loves her sweet, old aunt. Ain't that right, Miss James?"

He took her by the arm and started dragging her to the screen door. "Kill that old woman, Tyler!"

"No!" Samantha screamed as she was dragged out of the house.

Guy Stanley saddled Samantha's mare, while Zack Strickland prevented her from running inside to her aunt. At the sound of a gunshot she dropped to her knees and stared, stunned, at the kitchen door. Tyler Strickland sauntered out as though he'd just had lunch.

Too dazed to cry, she was tossed onto her horse, tied to the pommel, and led away.

Just outside of Logan, Max reined in his horse, his eyes skimming the dusty road beneath him. He wasn't sure how it had happened, but just inside the Nevada border the Stricklands had circled around on him and had headed back toward Logan in a damn big hurry. They couldn't be more than a half hour in front of him. His jaw tightened. He could feel the truth ripping at his gut. Somehow they'd found out where he'd taken Samantha, and she was going to be their revenge.

He took off toward town as if the devil were at his back. In record time he arrived at Ida's and found the house too quiet for his peace of mind.

He stepped onto the porch and in through the front door. The place was a wreck. The rocking chair had been splintered into pieces, a lamp was shattered all over the couch, and even the curtains had been torn from the front window.

He was afraid to see what might be awaiting him in the next room. Gathering his strength, he went into the kitchen.

"It's about damn time you showed up!"

Ida was sitting on the floor, her hands tied to the stove leg.

FAN THE FLAME 211

"What the hell kinda marshal are you, leaving two defenseless women alone to fend for themselves!"

"Where's Samantha?"

Tears flooded Ida's green eyes. "They took her."

He bent down and untied her hands. "Who? Who took her?"

"Those giant red-headed heathens! And that bastard son-of-a-gun Guy Stanley!"

Max paled. "Sheriff Stanley?"

"He's their cousin. Can you believe it!"

"Christ."

"They're only a few minutes in front of ya! Get the hell on that horse and go fetch my niece!"

Max exited through the kitchen door only to run smack dab into Pete Holden.

The young man looked startled, and a bit disappointed, Max noted. "You're back?"

Max mounted his horse. "Samantha's been kidnapped."

"Kidnapped! Are you going after her?"

"What the hell do you think, Holden?"

Max didn't like the determined look that came up in Pete Holden's eyes. "Then I'm going with you."

"The last thing I need is to have to baby-sit you."

Pete was already mounted up. He reached down and took the Winchester that Ida was handing up to him. "Thank you, Mrs. Olsen. You may not believe this, Marshal, but I am a crack shot."

Max snorted. "Really?"

Holden cocked the rifle, pointed it toward the barn, and shot a hole through the center of a pail fifty yards away. The pail flew into the air, Holden cocked the rifle again, and shot it before it hit the ground.

Max had to admit he was impressed. "I don't have time for this. If you want to come along I can't stop you, short of putting a bullet through your head. But if you get in my way, Holden, I'll shoot right through you."

24

Samantha's back was starting to ache. Her hands were tied to the pommel of her saddle, which prevented her from getting into a comfortable position for the fast uphill climb. They'd been traveling nonstop for two hours. She kept glancing behind her, hoping to see someone coming to her rescue. She had one Strickland in front of her and one Strickland behind. Guy Stanley had headed in the opposite direction, his work in Logan obviously finished.

"Bet you're wondering how we knew you and the marshal would be headin' for Logan," Tyler Strickland called from behind her. "It was your boyfriend. The one in Spokane Falls."

Randy. Samantha wished she'd had the courage to shoot him that day in her barn.

"I can see why he'd be gettin' drunk over losin' you—can you see why, Zack?"

"Yeah, but there's better things to get drunk over," the elder Strickland answered.

Tyler giggled. "Yeah. Like the death of a marshal."

"Pigs," Samantha muttered.

"What?" Zack Strickland turned at the waist to look back at her. "What did you say, lady?"

"I said you're both a couple of pigs!"

"I can live with that. Can you live with that, Tyler?"

"Hell, yeah! As long as we're happy pigs."

Zack Strickland pulled his horse back until he was riding alongside her. "And right now this pig is lookin' to find a comfy sow to settle himself into later. How 'bout you, Miss James? You a comfy sow?"

She kept her eyes straight ahead, refusing to look at him, afraid he might see the terror in her eyes.

He reached out a hand toward her brooch. "What ya got here?"

She turned her body, trying to keep him from getting a good look at the piece of jewelry, but he pulled her back toward him and ripped the brooch off her dress. Before he could pull his hand away, however, she sank her teeth into his wrist. He cried out in pain and then slapped her hard on the back of the head. She would have fallen off her saddle if her hands hadn't been tied to it.

"You just wait 'til we get to the canyon, honey. I'm gonna work you so hard, your pretty ass will be planted in the ground before I'm finished."

An hour later Samantha's hands were starting to go numb. She wiggled her fingers, trying to work the blood through them. The sudden squawking of a crow caught her attention, and she stole a quick glance into the trees behind her. Her breath caught. Max gave her a quick wave before darting back out of sight.

She faced forward. He was here. And he was going to save her.

Max hurried back to Holden.

"Did you see them?" Holden asked anxiously.

"She's safe for now."

"They're heading straight for Sardine Canyon. There's only one trail in."

Max mounted, wishing Pete Holden had stayed in Logan where he belonged. "Then I suppose we'll have to make ourselves another."

"Marshal, it's sheer mountain and rock all around that canyon. There is no other way in."

"If you can't cut it, I'm not forcing you to go." He kicked his horse forward.

Pete hesitated and then began following him again. "I sure hope you know what you're doing."

Max hoped the hell he did too. He'd gone for

almost a week without much sleep and a pain in his heart nobody should be forced to bear. And now they'd taken her, right out from under his nose. It was a delicate situation, one that, if he didn't keep his wits about him, might mean the loss of the only woman he'd ever loved.

Samantha stood next to her horse, rubbing her wrists where the rope had burned her skin. They'd ridden until the sky had purpled with the sunset, and stopped finally on a ridge in a high-walled canyon. The Stricklands were checking their rifles and all but ignoring their prisoner. In a horseshoe canyon, there was nowhere for Samantha to run.

She studied the landscape. She had a perfect view of the whole canyon from where she stood on the ridge. Mountainous walls shot up on either side of the lone trail below, and she knew that Max would never be able to ride in and make it back out alive. Samantha shivered. That was obviously what the Stricklands had in mind.

She heard an odd sound in the distance and could have sworn it was the tune of *Waltzing Matilda* being sung terribly. The voice grew louder and more painful to the ear, and she saw a rider entering the canyon in the distance.

"Dear Lord," she whispered. It was Pete Holden.

She watched in utter disbelief as an obviously

very drunk Pete, astride his faithful horse, wandered into the danger-filled canyon.

"Who the hell is that?" Zack Strickland squinted for a better view.

Tyler laughed. "Don't know, Zack, but he's a mighty happy hombre."

"That man's drunker than a club beaten bear."

Samantha shut her eyes and tried to wish Pete away.

"I sure could use me a taste of that rotgut," Tyler whispered to his brother. He licked his dry, cracked lips. "Should I ask 'im if he's got any more?"

Pete weaved precariously in the saddle, his voice still raised in poor pitch. "I don't need you gettin' drunk on me, Tyler."

"Aw, come on, Zack," Tyler said. "I'll only have me a little. 'Sides, once we get our hands on Barrett, it might come in handy in loosening the pretty lady up a bit."

Samantha watched Zack's eyes light up. She didn't know what was going on. Should she warn Pete away or be happy he was there? Could he possibly be coming to help her?

"Call the man up here, Tyler." Zack Strickland turned to her. "One word out of you and I'll blow this man's head off."

Pete urged his horse up the winding trail that led to the ridge. Samantha couldn't believe that Max would have let the drunken fool get by him, and that could only mean one thing: Pete was in on a plan of the marshal's.

Soon Pete reached their camp. "Got anymore a' that stuff with ya, Mister?" Tyler asked. "We sure would be grateful for a little taste."

"And jusss how grateful might you be?" Pete's words were slurred. He stopped his horse in front of them and practically fell out of the saddle. Then he stood, a bit unsteady on his feet. "I sssure could"—he hiccoughed—"ssure use me some coin."

"Oh, we got money. Right, Zack?"

"Sure, Mister." Zack turned to his brother and said, "This fella's so drunk, if we pushed him off a cliff he'd bounce."

While the Stricklands spoke with Pete, trying to get him to give up a bottle of what he was drinking, Samantha stole hidden glances at the mouth of the canyon, watching for Max. When she saw him her heart clenched with pride and fear. He was keeping himself remarkably well hidden as he moved along the trail of the canyon. His gray shirt and dusty-colored hair blended perfectly with the terrain of dirt, rocks, and gray-barked trees. But if either of the Stricklands saw him, it would all be over: his life, her life, and Pete's.

Tyler was getting impatient with Pete. "Look, Mister, either give us your goddamn rotgut or we're agonna take it from ya!"

Samantha turned to Pete, determined to stall to give Max more time to move into position. "You might as well give it to them. They're just going to kill you and take it anyway."

With a backhanded slap, Zack Strickland sent her to the ground. "You shut your mouth, bitch, or I'll stuff something in it!"

When Samnatha hit the ground she felt as if every bone in her body had disintegrated. But she climbed back to her feet, not wanting to take the chance that Pete would fall out of character to help her.

The Stricklands turned back to Pete, and Samantha risked another glance over her shoulder. Max was only fifty yards away, crouched behind a stand of trees. He was definitely in rifle range. She straightened her shoulders to let him know she was all right.

Her nerves began to tighten. She sensed that Pete was anxious, even though his eyes hadn't roamed her way since the painful slap.

A birdcall drifted softly on the air, and she noted a change in Pete's eyes. She got ready to run.

Suddenly Pete pulled a pistol out from under his jacket and shot Tyler Strickland in the chest. Then he stared at what he'd done, and the gun slipped out of his fingers.

Zack Strickland let out a violent roar and drew his gun on Pete. But Pete didn't move. As Zack Strickland thumbed the hammer on his gun, Samantha knew she had to do something fast.

* * *

Max had smiled in satisfaction when Pete fired his pistol. "One down, one to go." He took careful aim at Zack Strickland's massive chest. The plan was working perfectly.

Perfectly, that is, until Samantha darted in front of Max's sights.

25

Samantha rammed herself against Zack Strickland with all her might, hitting his gun with her outstretched arm and making it fire harmlessly in the air. Pete seemed to snap out of his daze for a moment, long enough to dive behind the trunk of a large tree.

Max swore under his breath. Just one more damn second, one more goddamned second, and it would have been over.

Zack Strickland wrapped his beefy arm around Samantha's neck and hauled her up against him. She clawed at his arm, and Zack yelled to Pete, "Come out of there or I'll blow her head off!"

From where Max was, he could see that Pete had no intention of budging. And Samantha's face was turning red from lack of air.

He stood, holding his shotgun level. "It's me you want, Strickland. Let the girl go."

Zack swung around to face Max and laughed in evil delight. His hold on Samantha tightened. "Barrett, you son-of-a-bitch. I shoulda known you'd pull somethin' like this."

"Let her go, Strickland."

"You put down the rifle or I'll snap her lovely neck."

"Kill her and you're next."

"You think I care about that? Hell, you've just murdered my entire family!" He yanked his arm tighter around Samantha's neck, and she grunted, her face now turning purple.

Max didn't have any choice. He had to make a deal. "You let her go, and I'll take you one on one, Strickland. Come on. Two big boys fightin' for the prize."

Zack hesitated. The thought of getting Max Barrett in his massive hands had to be appealing to him. "All right, Marshal, I'll let the little honey go. You just set your rifle over there a-ways and we'll get down to business."

Max fought the urge to glance at the thick tree where Pete Holden was hiding. He should have known he wouldn't be able to count on the young man. He backed up a few paces and set down his gun. Then he moved just out of reach of Zack Strickland. "Now let her go."

Strickland let out a hard laugh and pushed

Samantha away from him. She landed, dazed, a few feet away. Then he advanced toward Max, and the contest was on.

"I haven't decided yet how I'm gonna kill the little lady."

Max stayed just out of reach as they circled each other.

"Break her neck, strangle her, peel off her skin an inch at a time . . . Which do you prefer, Barrett?"

He swung, and Max avoided the punch, landing one of his own on Strickland's jaw. Then they both quickly moved apart again.

"I prefer a bullet. Like the one I put between your brother's eyes."

Zack snarled. "I'm gonna enjoy this, Barrett."

"Not half as much as I am."

With a bloodcurdling howl, Strickland charged him. Max got him with a right to the face and an uppercut to the kidney. Strickland went down, and Max landed on top of him. They rolled and punched and choked and jabbed, until God Himself wouldn't have been able to tell which limb belonged to which man.

And then, suddenly, Strickland had Max by the collar, with a knife pressed against his throat.

"You wiped out my entire family, you piece of shit lawman! And before I kill you I want you to know that I plan to do the same to yours!"

Sweat trickled into Max's eyes as he realized he

was going to die. His only hope was that Samantha would be spared this man's brutality, if Pete Holden would come to his senses and somehow save her. Then he saw Samantha rising to her feet. In her hand was the rifle he'd set on the ground.

"Let him go," she said in a low voice.

Zack laughed. "Is that your little honey I hear behind me, Barrett? She's a little spitfire, ain't she. I'm gonna have to tie her up before I have her."

Tears were streaming down Samantha's face. "God help me, you let him go or I'll shoot."

Strickland pressed the knife to Max's neck until Max felt a trickle of blood run down his throat. "You put that down, bitch, or loverboy here's a dead man."

"Looks to me like he's dead either way."

Max squeezed his eyes shut as the sound of the rifle blasted in his ears.

The recoil knocked Samantha backward. She landed, hard, on the ground and looked up to see Strickland lying on top of Max. Neither one was moving.

She jumped to her feet and ran to the men. Blood was pooling on the back of Zack Strickland's shirt. She used every ounce of her strength to roll the heavy outlaw off Max. Strickland's yellow eyes stared sightlessly up at her.

She turned her attention to Max, searching his still face. There was blood on his left shoulder.

"Max? Max, are you all right? Can you hear me? Max!"

She put her hands along the sides of his head to try and get his attention, and that was when she noticed the blood on her fingers. She turned his head and found a three-inch gash on the back of it. He'd struck a rock when he'd fallen.

"Pete! Help me! He's hit his head!"

Pete Holden finally edged out from behind the tree. "Is that yellow-eyed jackal dead?"

Samantha was nearly sobbing. "Yes. We've got to get the marshal to a doctor. Hurry! *Help me!*"

26

The only way to get Max down the mountain and back to Logan was to drape him over his saddle. Samantha balked at this idea at first, fearing it might injure Max more, but Pete convinced her it was the only way.

After two long hours during which she feared every jostle of Max's horse, they reached Logan, just before sunset.

Samantha had little energy to respond with more than a heartfelt smile when she found her aunt alive and well. Tyler Strickland apparently hadn't had the courage to shoot a woman who reminded him of his dead mother. A doctor came, and she, Pete, and Ida paced the kitchen, waiting for Max's prognosis.

Pete was still looking very pale. Ida had just seated

him at the table with a strong cup of coffee when the doctor came into the room.

"Took ten stitches to patch him up. Got himself a nasty smash on the head. By the way, he did get nicked by that bullet"—Samantha closed her eyes and sank down into a chair—"but that's the least of his problems. His pupils are dilated and uneven. He's completely unresponsive."

"When will he wake up?" Samantha asked tremulously.

"I'm afraid the longer he's out, Miss James, the worse his chances get."

Silent tears streamed down Samantha cheeks and she looked up to find that even Ida's eyes were damp. "What do we need to do?"

"Wait. That's all you can do. I'm sorry."

While Ida showed the doctor out, Samantha slipped down the hall and into her bedroom, where Max lay stretched out on the small bed. He had a bandage wrapped around his head and his shirt had been removed to wrap his shoulder wound. She sat down next to him and clasped his hand, noting that he still had the same warmth she'd come to associate with his touch. He looked as if he was sleeping and if she'd just shake him he'd wake up, open his blue eyes, and smile at her.

"Doc says to watch him for fever."

Samantha looked up as her aunt entered the room. "This is all my fault, Ida."

"Nonsense, Sammy. The man does this for a livin'. Gettin' shot up and knocked on the head is all part of the job. You wait. He's gonna wake up and tell you the exact same thing."

They both looked down expectantly at Max, but he didn't move—not even a flicker of his eyelids.

Ida scowled. "He's as stubborn as a mule."

"The longer he's unconscious the worse his chances are. God, I want to bring down the loudest thunder from heaven to wake him up and make him open his eyes!"

She covered her face as sobs shook through her. Ida pulled her up from the bed and wrapped her in her arms. "Ya gotta keep your head up, Sammy. That's what he'd want. I've heard that if you talk to people in these situations you can sometimes snap 'em out of it."

Samantha sniffed and wiped her eyes. "You better go see to Pete. Make sure he gets home all right."

"It's gettin' late, Sammy. Would you like me to fix ya something to eat?"

She looked down at Max. "I couldn't eat."

"You're gonna sit here and stare at him all night, aren't ya? You can't will him to wake up, Sammy. He'll open those blue peepers again when he's good and ready."

"I know. And don't worry, I'll get some rest tonight."

Ida left the room and shut the door. Samantha

checked Max's temperature, found his forehead cool, and pulled the blankets over him and up to his chin. Then she settled into a chair to wait.

The night wore on endlessly, and Max never moved. She paced the room to relieve the cramps in her legs from sitting, and stared out the window, whispering prayers toward the starry sky. Finally, just before dawn, she curled up beside Max on the bed and fell asleep.

Kitchen sounds woke Samantha later that morning. She opened her eyes and found she was sleeping with her arm draped over Max's chest and her head tucked into his neck. She sat up and peered into his face.

"Max?"

His blank expression didn't change.

"Max, can you hear me?"

She cupped his chin and ran her thumb over his moustache. He was still unconscious.

She slipped off the bed and left the room for the kitchen. Ida was standing at the stove, frying eggs. "Ready for breakfast, Sammy?"

"No, Ida. I have something to do this morning. I think I'll do it now before I lose my nerve."

"You're not thinkin' of teaching today, are ya?"

"No. I'll stop by Mrs. Strithright's and see if she can stand in for me for a few days. Then I plan to send a telegram to Max's family and tell them what's happened."

"Sammy, don't be jumpin' the gun—"

"Ida, if Max . . . if something goes wrong, the Barretts have every right to be here."

Ida hesitated. "You know how I hate puttin' the cart before the horse."

"Will you watch him while I'm gone?"

"You get on over to the telegraph office and do what you have to do, Sammy. If that marshal wakes up while you're gone I can give him the ear blisterin' he deserves."

Samantha took her shawl off a hook and went out the screen to come face to face with Pete Holden. His eyes were still vaguely haunted.

"Are you going to town, Miss James?"

"I'm sending a telegram to the Barretts this morning."

Pete paled. "He isn't . . ."

"No. I just feel the Barretts have a right to be here if he does. You look like you barely slept last night."

Pete hung his head. "I killed a man."

"Yes, Mr. Holden, you did. You killed a man who robbed and murdered for a living."

"Can the taking of any life truly be justified?"

"In the case of self-preservation and protecting the ones you love, yes, I believe it can."

"You love that marshal very deeply, don't you?"

A tear trembled on her lashes and slid down her cheek. "Yes."

"Is there anything I can do?"

"You can walk me to the telegraph office. I don't think my legs will support me the whole way."

He offered her his arm. "You may lean on me, Miss James."

After a quick stop at Mrs. Strithright's, Samantha found Mr. Beeman at his desk in the telegraph office. But when he asked her what, exactly, she wanted to say in the telegram to the Barretts of Carson City, she found herself at a loss. What do you tell a family whose son is on the brink of death? Pete Holden recited a very well-worded but urgently put message for her and then took her back to Ida's house.

They found Ida in the bedroom, explaining to a still unconscious Max how to make sweet cream out of the morning milk, apparently applying the theory she had heard about constant talking. After checking his temperature, Samantha sat back down in the chair to wait once again.

The day dragged on with little change. Many of the people in town came to pay their respects. Some brought by food, but Samantha still couldn't make herself eat more than a thin slice of cheese. By the time darkness fell she was so weak that Ida forced her to eat some soup. And then, once again, Samantha curled up next to Max to ride out the long night.

Max opened his eyes and frowned at the darkened room. He turned to the woman snuggled up next to him, trying to remember what she was doing there. "Samantha?"

She curled up closer to him and whispered sleepily, "Hmm?"

"I really need a bowl of sweet cream."

She opened one eye and frowned at him. "At this hour—Oh, good Lord, you're awake!"

The sound of her squeal sent a throbbing through his head, and he groaned. "Christ, I have a wicked headache."

She touched his face and smiled. "You're not hot."

He grinned back at her. "Says who?"

Samantha leapt up from the bed and lit a lamp. "I'm not dreaming this, am I? You wouldn't do that to me, right?"

He arched a brow at her. "I think you might be a little dazed. Maybe you should come back over here and lie down a little longer."

"Ida!" she yelled. "Ida, come quick!"

A few moments later Ida came lumbering into the room, wrapping her housecoat around her. "Why looky there!" she cried. "The rascal's finally decided to grace us with his full attention."

"I'm not dreaming, am I, Aunt Ida?"

"Not unless I am too. And having him prancing through my nighttime pleasures is not something I care to think about."

Max sat up in the bed. He winced and touched his head, skimming his fingers over the thick bandage. Then he noticed the one on his arm. "Somebody care to tell me what the hell's going on?"

Samantha seemed unable to stop smiling. "You hit your head."

"You appear to be awfully happy about that."

"No, I'm happy you're finally awake."

"Finally?"

"You hit yer head and have been out for almost two straight days," Ida said.

Startled, Max looked down at his shoulder. "And this?"

A blind man couldn't have missed Samantha's flush.

"Don't tell me. You finally shot me?"

"I certainly didn't mean to," she said. "I shot Strickland—in order to save your life, by the way—and the bullet sort of passed through him and nicked your shoulder."

He flexed his arm and felt a strong burn. "It doesn't feel like a nick."

"Well for cryin' out loud. Just look at all that gratitude pouring out of him. You sure you can stand all these thank-yous, Sammy?"

"How's Strickland?"

"Dead."

Max nodded. "And Pete?"

Ida let out a laugh. "His humiliation over the whole matter of hiding behind that tree has been eatin' at him, but he's fine otherwise. Although he's actin' like he shot Rutherford B. Hayes himself. You hungry?"

"Yeah."

"A big slice of pie?"

He smiled. "Smothered in sweet cream?"

Ida and Samantha exchanged looks and started laughing.

27

Samantha hurried toward the telegraph office with a certain skip to her stride. Max was up and moving about. The doctor had given him a clean bill of health that afternoon. This telegram she would have no problem wording on her own. She only hoped the Barretts weren't already on their way to Logan.

Just as she passed the mercantile the stage rolled into town, and she couldn't help but stare. It was piled high with more pieces of luggage than she'd ever seen in her life. She waited in front of the telegraph office to see who would alight, sensing with trepidation that she already knew who it would be.

A man stepped down from the Wells Fargo stage, and Samantha had her hunch confirmed. He was an exact replica, although twenty years older, of Max

Barrett. He helped down a woman of middle years who was wearing a stylish blue dress with matching hat. This would probably be Mrs. Barrett. Then came another woman, this one older and gray-haired and stooped over a black cane. As the elder Mr. Barrett procured all the many pieces of luggage, two other women stepped down, one a younger version of Mrs. Barrett, and the other a pale-haired woman dressed in the flounciest pink dress Samantha had ever seen.

Not knowing what else to do, she approached them. "Hello. I don't suppose you'd be the Barretts?"

The old woman leaned on her cane and snorted. "The better part of us would be."

The pale-haired woman grimaced and shook out her pink dress. "And who might you be?"

"I'm Samantha James. I'm the person who wired you about Marshal Barrett."

Five pairs of concerned eyes fell upon her, and she smiled. "I'm happy to tell you that Max finally woke up last night and is doing much better today. The doctor says—"

"Max?" the blond woman echoed, giving Samantha a strange look.

"Yes, Camille," the other young woman said. "That is my brother's name."

"She seems to know it well enough, wouldn't you say, Frances?"

Max's mother nodded. "Where is my son?"

"He's staying with my aunt and me—"

"Staying with you and your aunt?" the woman named Camille exclaimed. "Why isn't he in a hospital? Surely this backwards hovel has a hospital?"

"Camille, please," Mr. Barrett said. "The young lady said he's awake and moving around today. I'm sure Max is just fine."

"Just fine?" Mrs. Barrett repeated. "This woman greeted us yesterday morning with a telegram stating more or less that our son was on his deathbed. How fine could he be today?"

"Very fine. You can see for yourself if you like. My aunt's house is just down the street and to the left. It's blue with—"

"Thank you." Camille stuck her nose in the air, linked arms with Max's mother, and strode off down the street. Mr. Barrett quickly hired a few bystanders to help him with the numerous pieces of luggage and followed after them.

Dumbfounded, Samantha turned back to the only two people left: the old woman and Max's sister. "I don't suppose you'd like me to show you the way?"

"Do you see what I see, Brandon?" the old woman asked the younger one.

The younger nodded. "I noticed it right away. What do you think it means?"

"Exactly what it's supposed to mean. What it's meant for a hundred years."

Both women smiled, and Samantha decided that the whole family was off its rocker. They were staring at the front of her dress, and she looked down to see what all the fuss was about. The gold brooch flashed in the early afternoon sunshine. Fortunately, she'd remembered to retrieve it from Zack Strickland's pocket.

"That's a lovely piece of jewelry," Max's sister said. "Where did you get it?"

Samantha touched the brooch. Max had said it had been in his family for years. Could these two women resent her wearing it and demand to have it returned? "It was a gift."

"I don't suppose you'd care to tell us the circumstances in which it was given?" the old woman asked.

"Not particularly, no."

The young woman broke into a broad smile. "She's got spunk, Grandmother."

"Yes. I'm noticing that. I am Moriah Barrett, and this is my sometimes delightful granddaughter Brandon."

Brandon scowled good-naturedly at her grandmother. "We are very pleased to make your acquaintance, Samantha James."

Moriah Barrett linked arms with Samantha and began to walk down the street in the direction the others had gone. "Tell me, my dear, how long have you known my grandson?"

"Has my brother told you anything about Camille St. Clair?"

Samantha was becoming more and more confused. "About two months and, no, I don't think so. Was she the woman in the pink dress?"

"What do you think is going on, Grandmother?"

"How the devil should I know. But I do, however, have a feeling that things are about to get very interesting."

Max watched in shock as his parents, along with Camille St. Clair, barged in through the front door of Ida Olsen's house. "What the hell is going on here?"

His mother gave him a tight hug. "We were sent word that you were gravely injured, Maxwell." She touched the bandage on his head. "How are you?"

Max glared at Ida, who was standing in the kitchen doorway, looking as if she'd been invaded by the British. "I am fine, Mother. It wasn't necessary for you to travel all the way here to Logan."

"And when would you have come to see us?" Camille demanded.

When you dropped off the face of the earth, he wanted to say to her. "As a matter of fact, when I was finished with my business here, I was planning on visiting for a little while."

"Really? And what is your business here, Max?"

"Yes, Maxwell," his mother said. "Who is this woman, and this Samantha James?"

"This is Ida Olsen, who's been kind enough to let me stay at her house for a while, and Samantha is her niece and the daughter of an old friend of mine—"

"She's in love with you," Camille interrupted him.

"Excuse me?"

"She's in love with you. It's written all over her plain little face. Have you told her about us?"

"No, I haven't told her about us—"

"Maxwell, you shouldn't tamper with the feelings of a young woman in this way. The poor girl is bound to be heartbroken when you and Camille—"

"When me and Camille nothing, Mother. Nothing has been decided. Now, I really have a roaring headache. Could you just go settle into a hotel and discuss this with me later?"

"But it's such an interesting topic," Samantha said, coming in through the front door. "Do go on, Mrs. Barrett. When Camille and Maxwell what?"

"Why, when they marry, of course."

Max wanted to strangle his mother for saying that when he saw the stricken look in Samantha's eyes. "Mother, please—"

"They've been planning it for years, since they were children."

Max couldn't bear to look at Samantha's face any longer. Her tone of voice was enough to tell him her state of mind. "How wonderful for them. If you'll excuse me, I have some things to do in my room."

Max reached for her as she passed by him, but she shrugged off his hand. The slam of her door was the most painful sound he'd ever heard. He gave his mother a murderous glare and left the house for the barn.

His grandmother and, unfortunately, Ida followed him.

"Hold on there just one second, fella!" Ida shouted.

Max stopped inthe barn doorway.

"I just wanted to tell you that you are *the* lowest, *the* shabbiest, *the* most irrefutable bastard this side of the sun!"

"Wait just a minute there, woman," his grandmother said. "I'll not have you talking to my grandson that way." She turned to him with a proprietary look. "Only I'm allowed to do that. Well? Speak up for yourself, boy. We're all ears. What the hell have you been doing to that poor girl in there?"

"Which poor girl would that be, Grandmother?"

"Don't mince words with me. You know how I feel about that Camille St. Clair. That woman is a finagler, a plotter, a manipulator, and I don't want her in my family!"

"Sounds to me like the two of 'em were made for each other," Ida said.

"You've been having serious thoughts about this Samantha girl, haven't you, Maxwell Barrett—and don't say no, I saw the brooch with my own two eyes."

"It was a present."

"As it should be. But you and I both know what the giving of that brooch is supposed to mean. Camille's been waiting forever for you to give it to her, pouting every Christmas and every birthday when she doesn't get the thing."

"He gave it to Sammy on her birthday."

"Along with a marriage proposal, I hope—"

"Not on yer life, old woman. I don't want this fella in my family any more than you want that high-nosed she-devil in yours."

Max felt his anger rising again. "Ida here has got a decent man all picked out for her niece."

"That's right. A real nice fella, with a town business, a good heart, and a stable home."

"Everything I'm lacking."

His grandmother eyed him. "I'm surprised you're letting *this* woman stop you from getting what you want, my boy. When your mother appealed directly to the government to reject your application for marshal, that didn't stop you from enlisting. When Camille tried to spring a surprise wedding on you last October, that didn't stop you from embarrassing yourself and your family by leaving her at the altar. Is this Ida woman really that daunting?"

"But she's right, Grandmother. I can't give Samantha everything she needs. She's better off with Holden."

"Good God, how I hate martyrs. Has anyone ever thought to ask Samantha what she wants? What makes you two think the girl will automatically choose this Holden man just because she doesn't get Max Barrett. Perhaps she'll live her life in misery wishing for what never was. Perhaps she'll blame you, Mrs. Olsen, for preventing her from fulfilling her heart's desire."

"I'm not standin' in Sammy's way—"

Moriah stamped her cane. "You most certainly

are! You've talked this boy into believing he's not fit to shine your niece's shoes. And I, for one, plan to make sure Samantha knows it."

Max could only shake his head and shrug. His grandmother wasn't known for playing fair.

"But he's a marshal," Ida protested. "He's gonna run off and leave my Sammy alone for months on end. Just look at how long it's been since you've seen him!"

"A lot of that has to do with my brave young man here avoiding the enchantress Camille. That's also one reason he enlisted as a U.S. Marshal. Well, my boy? Have you run from the inevitable long enough? Are you ready to settle down and make yourself a respectable family man?"

"Not with Camille, I'm not."

Moriah looked at him intently. "Then I suppose the real question is, do you love Samantha James enough to make her happy?"

28

Samantha stared, in a daze, at the pink floral wallpaper of her bedroom. She fidgeted with the fringe on the bedspread, trying to keep herself from crying uncontrollably and fighting the urge to climb out the window and run into the wilderness. She didn't think she could bear to face any of the Barretts or her aunt ever again.

A knock came at the door, and Moriah Barrett shuffled into the room without waiting for permission. "I brought you something to munch on, my dear. You're looking very pale."

Samantha wiped the tears from her face. "That's because I've sat up the past two nights nursing your underhanded grandson. I never want to set eyes on that man again."

"Yes. I suppose if I were you I'd want to sock him straight in the nose myself. Especially if I had your history with men."

Samantha blinked. "Excuse me?"

"Your aunt told me all about your two former beaux. Sad stories each of them. Oughta put them in a book."

"I don't want my misfortunes plastered over the pages of a book. I've got enough problems without the whole world knowing what a fool I am!" Her tears began to flow again.

Moriah set the plate of cookies on the table by the bed. "You know, if you could stop crying for just ten seconds, young lady, you and I might get along famously."

"I'm sorry," Samantha whispered. "I don't think I've ever c-cried this much in my life!"

Moriah handed her a silk handkerchief. "Blow your nose and tell me what you plan to do about Max and Camille."

"Do?" She laughed. "I'm not going to come in between Max and his *true love*."

Moriah snorted. "I know *he* didn't tell you that."

"His mother said it all. They've been planning to marry for years. Why didn't he tell me?"

The woman pointed a sharp finger at her. "Don't you start wailing again, young lady, or I'll turn around and leave this room. If you're wearing that brooch then I know you're made of stronger stuff than this. The first thing you need to know is not to pay any attention to a thing Frances Barrett says. She's a nose-pusher—a busybody. She's never had any idea as to what her son wants or feels—and I'll tell you something, missy, it sure isn't love he feels for that Camille St. Clair.

"Secondly," Moriah continued, "iIgnore that high-nosed blonde in the stupid pink dress. She's bound to lead you wrong at every turn. Camille has been after Max Barrett since she could say the word money. That's right, she's a gold digger. And she's going to do everything she can to stop you from taking that boy away from her. Any questions?"

Samantha shook her head, trying to follow what the woman was saying.

"As for Brandon, well, you can count on that one. She's hated that woman for some time now. She'll help you any way she can." The woman leaned on her cane, pressing her pointy nose closer. "Brandon likes you, ya know."

"Well, that's very nice, but—"

"Now, the really big obstacle is bound to be Max himself. He's gotten it into his head that he's not good enough to eat your leftovers."

"That's ridic—"

Moriah raised her frail hand. "Needless to say, he's decided this Holden fellow with a business and security would make you a better man."

"I told him Pete and I are nothing but—"

"Regardless of anything else, Max has never had any intention of marrying Camille St. Clair. He's never even considered it."

"He hasn't?"

"But he feels that you deserve the best, and that the best isn't him. Before this is over you may have to play your trump card."

"My trump card?"

"Yes, your trump card," Moriah repeated. "Young lady, haven't you been listening to a word I've said?"

"Yes, but I—"

"If Max decides to take for the hills once again, which wouldn't surprise me in the least, the boy's so thick-headed, you might have to tell him he got you with child."

Samantha leapt up from the bed. "What!"

"My grandson can be quite the seducer, so don't try to deny it, my dear. He's an honorable man. He'll do the honorable thing."

"I will not force Max to marry me by lying to him! This is ridiculous, all this 'trust this person' and 'watch out for that person.' I'm about to lose my mind just trying to keep up with you!"

Moriah grinned broadly. "Exciting, isn't it?"

Max dumped the luggage on the floor inside the hotel suite. His father followed with his own armful of suitcases, and then his mother and Camille sauntered in.

"You'll be comfortable enough here," he said.

"And where are you planning to stay?" Camille

asked, one eyebrow arched in the most irritating way.

"I've developed a fondness for barns."

Camille's blue eyes widened. "You're going to be staying with *her*."

"Maxwell, I hardly think—"

"That's right Mother, you don't. I still don't understand what the hell you're doing here. Since when does a little knock to the head constitute a twenty-four hour train ride? I've been injured before. You usually just sit tight and wait for further developments."

Camille and his mother exchanged a look. His father cleared his throat. "Camille was distressed about the young lady who sent the telegram, son. She felt it was in her best interest to come to Logan and take care of you herself."

"Take care of me? She couldn't cleanse a knee scrape—even if she ever had the inclination. So Camille gets a bee up her butt and the rest of you follow along behind her?"

"Maxwell, I couldn't very well let Camille come here to this untamed town alone."

Max nodded. "And with you along she'd have a better chance of convincing me to marry her before I take another breath of freedom. And what about you, Father? And Grandmother and Brandon?"

"You know your sister, son. Brandon refused to let Camille and your mother come and gang up against you. She insisted that she ride along to even things out. And I couldn't very well let all these women travel alone, so . . . here I am. Of course your grandmother wanted to come to watch all the fireworks."

"Well, there aren't going to be any fireworks. I'm going to say this one time and one time only. The wedding is off—Christ, it was never on!"

His mother gasped. "What? But we've been planning it for years!"

"Yes, you've been planning it. Assuming I'd comply. I'm not going to, Mother. I never will."

"You can't do this!" Camille shouted. "I've waited forever for you, and you can't just—"

"Watch me! If you've done any waiting it's been because of your own stubbornness. I never gave you any indication that I'd be marrying you—ever!"

His mother glared. "You're going to marry that James girl, aren't you!"

"That decision has yet to be made."

"She's just a penniless small-town teacher, Maxwell. She can't bring a thing to a marriage."

Max looked down at his mother, regretting that she could never accept him for what he was: a simple man who didn't want money or a fancy house. "What she could bring, Mother, is happiness, love, and warmth. That's all the wealth I need."

29

Brandon poked her head into Samantha's room, her dark hair spilling into her blue eyes. "How's it going?" she asked her grandmother.

Moriah snorted. "Not well." She glared at Samantha, and Samantha glared right back. "The girl is still refusing to come out for dinner. Frankly, I don't understand it. I would have expected her to have more backbone than this."

Brandon laughed and came all the way into the room. "You're probably intimidating her with all your scowling, Grandmother. Honestly, the woman's had quite a shock. It might help if you stop putting so much pressure on her."

Samantha smiled gratefully at Brandon. "Thank you."

"After all, how is she to understand that we're

struggling to oust an overbearing, high-nosed witch from our midst? Why should she care that Max is doomed to spend the rest of his life with a domineering hag?"

Samantha looked at Brandon in shock. Now they were ganging up on her? "I am not going out there and humiliating myself in front of your whole family and this witch Camille. I've had enough. I've finally learned my lesson with men and will not subject myself to any further embarrassment."

"Bah! The girl's right. The boy couldn't possibly love her."

Samantha didn't know whether to be relieved or heartbroken when Brandon nodded in agreement. "I suppose she's just been another one of my brother's many women. We should have seen it from the start." She gave Samantha a sympathetic look. "He's a cold-hearted man. Always using women and tossing them by the wayside."

"That boy's never done a thing for anybody else in his entire life."

"That's not true," Samantha said. "He's risked his life many times protecting me. Once I got lost in the mountains, and he spent hours searching for me, and he didn't give up, even when he'd thought for sure I'd drowned in the river. At night he kept me warm, during the day he kept me fed. And when I was kidnapped he"—her eyes burned with tears—"he gave himself up to Zack Strickland in my place."

Her mouth snapped shut when she saw the pleased grins on Moriah's and Brandon's faces. Thinking over the things she'd just said, they certainly didn't sound like the actions of a man who didn't care for her.

"He loves you, Samantha," Brandon said.

She wiped her tears. "But he's never told me that."

"Have you ever told him?"

Samantha shook her head.

"You listen to me, young lady. Are you going to let this man slip through your fingers? My grandson is the strongest, bravest man I know, but you've got him scared half out of his wits. He doesn't know whether to kiss you or run from you! And you love him, dammit! Are you going to fight for him, or just hand him over to someone who doesn't deserve him?"

Samantha listened to all this, struggling between following her heart, which said she loved Max endlessly, and her head, which said she'd had enough of male duplicity. She hadn't really fought to keep Ty or Randy—probably because she hadn't ever really loved them. But Max . . . she loved Max with her whole heart and soul. She couldn't stand the thought of trying to live without him. Moriah was right. She had to fight.

"What would it hurt for you to come to dinner and talk to him?" Brandon asked.

Samantha lifted her chin. It might hurt her pride a great deal, but she was going to do it.

* * *

Samantha filled her plate with food and sat down in the sitting room in a chair directly across from Camille. Max hadn't come into the house yet. She was going to waste away and die if he didn't really love her.

Max's family was seated in the kitchen; she and Camille were the only ones in the sitting room. Camille was staring down at her plate, picking daintily at her fried chicken.

Samantha self-consciously tucked a stray piece of hair behind her ear. She wondered what Ida had been thinking to invite all these people to supper. She wondered where Max was.

"The food is delicious," Brandon spoke up from the kitchen table.

The moments of silence that followed only served to heighten the tension in the room.

"Don't you think the food is delicious, Camille?" Brandon asked.

"It's hard to get a proper taste while balancing the plate on my legs," Camille grumbled. "A decent table would have been nice."

"We'll be sure to order ya one just as soon as possible," Ida replied.

More silence ensued, but Brandon was determined to fill the void. "I understand you're a teacher, Samantha. How many students do you have?"

"Thirty-five."

"How awful," Camille remarked. "Children give me hives."

"On purpose," Brandon said.

"Your manners are slipping with age, Brandon Barrett. You are supposed to give respect to your elders."

"Ah yes, you are getting a little long in the tooth, aren't you, Camille?"

Samantha bit her lip to keep from smiling as Camille shot the younger Barrett a glare. "I certainly don't have to put up with this kind of behavior while eating a greasy meal in a shack in the middle of nowhere!"

"Brandon," Frances Barrett said, "leave Camille alone."

"You don't have to put up with a dag-blammed thing," Ida replied. "You can get your baggy bunch of bones up off my couch and leave."

The screen door creaked open, and Max came into the kitchen. He was wearing a white shirt and the same buckskin pants he'd fished in while in Spokane Falls. Samantha's heart began to slam against her ribs.

"Oh, Maxwell you know how I hate it when you dress like a savage," Mrs. Barrett remarked.

"Those trousers really are very awful," Camille agreed.

Samantha shook her head in disbelief, and Max focused his attention on her. "Miss James."

"Mr. Barrett."

Once their eyes locked she found she couldn't look away. She felt as if she was drowning in a warm blue ocean. Suddenly all her anger and all her hurt of the past few hours washed away, and she wanted to throw herself into his strong arms.

Moriah cleared her throat, and Max broke the stare. "Fill yourself a plate, my boy. It's help yourself tonight."

"I'd avoid the chicken," Camille remarked.

Ida scowled, and Samantha decided she'd held her tongue long enough. "Miss St. Clair, there is a restaurant in town if you'd care to eat someplace else."

Camille gave her a haughty look. "No thank you, Miss James. I wouldn't want to abandon the rest of you."

"Oh, we won't even notice you're gone. I promise."

Moriah cackled from her place at the table, and Brandon burst out laughing. Camille turned to Max's mother for support. "Frances, do you want me to leave?"

"Not at all, Camille."

Camille gave Samantha a triumphant look, and Samantha almost expected the woman to stick out her tongue.

Max passed between them and took the chair against the wall. He settled his plate on his lap and looked up at Samantha. "So, what did I miss?"

"Miss?"

"While I was gone. Did school start off all right?"

"Yes. I was just telling Brandon that I have thirty-five students. They're a handful, but they're very eager to learn."

"Thirty-five? That's pretty good. They must all be turning out to get a look at the pretty new teacher."

He smiled, and Samantha felt her face grow warm. She heard a grunt from Camille but ignored it.

"How's your head?" She noticed he'd taken off the bandages and the sling on his arm.

"Better. But there's this certain voice"—he darted a glance at Camille—"that sends it pounding like hell."

"If you'd like, Max, I can give you one of my special scalp massages," Camille said. "Remember how I used to sit on your lap and relax you by running my fingers through your hair?"

A knot formed in Samantha's stomach. She looked up to find Max frowning.

"It's been a long time since I was thirteen," he said.

"Well, surely you remember the time you took me riding through that field of wild daisies outside of town. It was the most romantic day of my life."

"Yes, I remember that well. You told me you'd been exposed to the pox and needed to wash yourself off with fresh air. One of your better ploys."

"Ploy? A ploy is what this poor Samantha girl has been for you—a ploy to get my attention. Well, you've got it, Mr. Barrett!"

"Camille, the last thing in the world I want is your attention."

Samantha was watching the pair with barely concealed glee. Moriah hadn't been telling tales. Max really didn't care for this woman.

"I will not air our laundry in front of this . . . this person!"

Samantha didn't have to look up from her chicken to know Camille's comment pertained to her.

"We don't have laundry, Camille. Just a lot of mismatched socks," Max said.

"Oh, but you have so much more with this girl, is that it, Max? How much more, or should we all guess?"

"Careful, Camille."

"Careful? What, you don't want me voicing what we've all been thinking since we stepped off the stage and this bumpkin was there to greet us?"

Samantha wiped her face with her napkin and stood. "I, for one, would love to hear what you've been thinking. But instead of disturbing everyone else's meals, how about if you and I go outside and finish this discussion, Miss St. Clair?"

"Gladly, Miss James."

Samantha excused herself and led the way out the door and toward the barn, with Camille not far behind her.

Camille chose to take the offensive right away. "You're not going to get him!"

"And, apparently, neither are you."

"I won't give him up!"

"Camille, there's something I don't understand. What is the appeal of clinging to a man who doesn't want you?"

"He does want—"

"He doesn't. I was sitting right there not ten seconds ago when he made that very clear. You're a lovely woman. By holding onto this fantasy you're only hurting yourself. Don't you want children, a home?"

"I—Yes, of course I do!"

"Then why are you wasting your time on a man who isn't going to give you those things?"

"You're just trying to mix me up so you can have him!"

"No. I'm just trying to make you see that no man is worth ruining your life over. If the answer is clear that you have no future with him, it's time to move on. Find yourself someone who deserves your love, who loves you in return."

Camille narrowed her eyes suspiciously. "What do you care about my life?"

"I know how badly it hurts to have a man stomp on your heart."

The two of them stood silently for a moment before Camille said quietly, "I know he doesn't love me. And I'm old and wasted."

"No, you're young and vital. Any man would be a fool not to take a second look at you."

Her head shot up. "Any man but Max."

"You can't make a man love you. I know that from experience, believe me. And pursuing Max is only going to make the two of you miserable."

"You want him."

It was a statement, not a question, and Samantha wasn't about to lie. "I love him."

"He loves you too, I can tell—and he gave you that damned brooch."

Samantha glanced down at the pin, which was in its customary place on her bodice. "What is it about this piece of jewelry that causes such emotion in you people?"

"He didn't tell you?"

"No. He just said it was a family heirloom and that he wanted me to have it."

"It's normally part of a proposal, Miss James. Instead of rings, the Barrett men have always given the brooch. It means he intends to marry you."

Realization struck Samantha, along with a sudden burst of anger. She looked toward the house to see Max standing on the porch.

"Everything O.K. out here?"

Samantha reached up and pulled the brooch from her dress and stormed over to him. "Explain this!"

Max stared at the brooch in her hand and then at Camille across the yard. "It was a gift."

"Yes, and I understand now that it is intended to be a whole lot more! Was this your way of branding me before you left, Mr. Barrett? Your way of being sure you'd always have a claim on me in some twisted sort of way?"

"The damn thing was a gift, and I gave it to you because I didn't think you'd put as much stock as my family does in a stupid piece of jewelry."

"But you knew what it meant!" She slammed the brooch into his hand. "You gave me half a promise, you bastard, and that's just plain cowardly!"

The rest of the Barretts were beginning to emerge on the porch.

"Maybe I figured Mr. Holden would provide the other half."

"Oh, I am so tired of hearing you snivel about Pete Holden . . ."

"Snivel?"

"He's just your excuse for leaving me! You can't face the truth. That's been our problem all along!"

"And what is the truth, Miss James?"

"That you love me, dammit! And I love you!"

No one said a word. And then the sound of horses trotting into the yard broke the silence.

"Well, it's about time ya got here," Ida said, bustling toward the two men. "We was about to have bloodshed right here all over my grass!"

Pete tipped his hat at Samantha as he climbed down from his mount. He, Ida, and another shorter man approached Max.

"Marshal Barrett, this here is Mayor Bartholomew Stevens. I think he has a word or two to say to you."

The mayor doffed his bowler hat, revealing a thin layer of gray hair, and cleared his throat. "Mr. Barrett? Marshal Barrett. I have been instructed by the town council to offer you the prestigious position of Sheriff of Cache County."

The porch erupted into murmurs, and Samantha's heart jumped. If he accepted the position that would mean he'd be staying, right here in Logan.

Max's eyes turned cold. "Was this your idea?" he asked her.

"No, but I happen to think it's wonderful."

"I won't be coerced into staying, Samantha."

She shook her head and then walked past him toward the door. "Don't flatter yourself, Marshal," she said over her shoulder as she went into the house. "I wouldn't waste my valuable time trying to talk you into anything."

The sound of the screen door slamming tightened Max's nerves. His grandmother came forward and stomped her cane on the wooden porch. "Well, boy, you're a bigger dunderhead than I ever believed."

"Samantha had nothin' to do with this," Ida said. "It was me and your granny's idea."

"And you just blew it to hell," his grandmother added.

Max ran a hand through his hair. He didn't know what he was doing anymore. Maybe that fall on the rock had finally jarred his brain loose, and it was only downhill from here.

Suddenly another horse came pounding into the yard. "Mayor Stevens!" a young man shouted. "We got trouble! It's Sheriff Stanley! He's back in town! And he's shootin' everything in sight!"

30

Max left his horse at the far end of Main Street and headed toward the center of town. He could hear shots being fired in the distance, and he hoped the people of Logan had had enough sense to clear the area.

He moved forward cautiously, careful to stay on the soft dirt of the street where the sound of his footsteps were muffled. He passed the gun and barber shop and saw Guy Stanley standing in front of the haberdashery across the street. The man was in the process of shooting out the establishment's windows.

"Stanley!" he called from behind the shelter of a post.

Guy Stanley spun around, his pistol cocked and ready. "Who'sss there!"

Max watched Guy practically stumble over his own feet. Then he relaxed and moved out a little from the post. It was pretty apparent that Stanley was drunk off his ass. "You got a problem with those particular windows?"

Stanley peered through the darkness. "Who iss 'at?"

"It's Marshal Barrett."

The man broke into laughter. "Nah. Can't be Barrett. He'sss dead."

"Sorry to disappoint you, but I've got more lives than either one of us cares to live."

"Can't be Barrett!" the man shouted back. "My cousssins took care a that justice ssseekin' sss . . . that jusstice sseekin' ssson-of-a-bitch."

"Hate to be the bearer of bad news, but you don't have any cousins anymore."

Stanley pushed his hat back on his head with the tip of his gun. "That mean I'm not sheriff anymore?"

"Doubt it."

"Wull, wait a second. You killed *all* my cousssins?"

"Can't take credit for every single one, but I suppose I had a hand in each particular situation."

"Then that meanss I gotta kill you," Stanley returned, weaving slightly.

Max leaned back against a hitching post in full view of Guy Stanley. "Let me get this straight. You're about as steady as a windmill, blinder than a one-eyed bat, and you're planning on settling a debt with me?"

"That's about the gissst of it."

"Well, I hope you don't take offense at this, Stanley, but what little brain you've got is pickled solid green. You even point that gun in my direction and you're a dead man. That means you won't be wakin' up in the morning with a headache wondering what happened, you just plain won't be waking up."

"Don't you threaten me, Marshal! Why, I'll come right over there and punch you sssquare . . . sssquare in the faccce."

"And which one of my faces would that be? The one on the left, or the one on the right?"

"But I . . . I . . ."

To Max's great amazement the man began to cry. He lowered his gun, hunched his shoulders, and sobbed. "I ain't got nobody left. Nobody a'tol."

"If you ask me, you never had much of anybody to begin with."

Stanley's head snapped up. "What do you know about kin! Sssurely you were born sstraight out a hell! Thosse fellass raised me from nothin'—"

"And made you into nothing."

"They were my family! A man can't live without connect . . . without connectionsss!"

Guy Stanley sank down to the ground, his head bowed, and Max felt a pang of something for him. Here was this thieving dog of a man, crying his eyes out over the loss of his "connections." It was a sorry day indeed when an upstanding man of the law learned something about life from a fellow who valued it about as much as a clod of dirt.

He crossed the street and hefted Stanley up by the arm. "Relax, Stanley. Where you're going you're bound to make lots of connections. As for me, let's just hope it's never too late to start over."

Samantha sat in the chair in her room wondering if she'd ever find the courage to get into the bed in which Max had lain wounded only the night before. He'd been given a clear opportunity to stay with her, and he'd made another choice.

Tears slipped silently down her face, and she was glad Moriah hadn't decided to barge in on her again. Maybe she needed to let her emotions go, see if she couldn't cry Max Barrett out of her heart once and for all.

She heard a tap on the window and looked to the pulled curtains. Max was outside, staring in at her, and she felt a chill of apprehension crawl up her spine. He was leaving. Why else would he choose not to come inside?

She wiped her eyes and stood up to open the sash. She sat on the sill to let the night air cool her sense of panic, but couldn't bring herself to look at the man she loved.

"Did you catch Mr. Stanley?" she asked, her eyes riveted to the bedpost.

Max cleared his throat. "Yes."

There was a moment of silence—the kind that used to make her feel nervous and insecure but now just left her empty inside.

"Are you all right?" she finally asked him.

"Yes."

Another pause, and then, "You had something you wanted to say?" She wished he'd just say goodbye and leave.

"I wanted to apologize for accusing you earlier on the porch. Ida and my grandmother told me that you had nothing to do with Mayor Stevens's offer. I suppose when I feel cornered I tend to strike without thinking."

As an untamed animal should, she thought regretfully. "You're forgiven," she whispered. Her emotions were trying to take over, but she pushed them back down. "Is that all?"

"I wish you'd look at me, Samantha."

She caught a sob before it passed her lips. "I wish you'd leave and get it over with, Mr. Barrett."

"All my life I've been running from people, from any kind of connection, claiming I haven't wanted to be tied down. The truth is, I've been running from life. And I'm tired of it. I'm tired of being a coward."

She turned her eyes on him. "You're not a coward."

"Oh, I am. You had me pegged earlier. When it comes to dying I'm a real hero, but when it comes to living I'm damn solid yellow."

"Does this mean you'll be visiting your family more often?" She couldn't help hoping that he'd visit her on his way to see them, even though she knew she'd never be happy seeing him only occasionally.

He nodded. "More often than before."

"They'll be glad to hear it. I know your mother's rigid, but she loves you and only wants the best for you."

A slow smiled lifted his moustache. "Only you would defend my mother, Samantha, after the way she's treated you."

"She's a mother. Mothers are supposed to be protective."

He was still smiling, his eyes bright, and he leaned forward on the sill. "Can I come in?"

She stood and backed away. "I don't think that's a good idea."

He slipped his long legs in through the window and climbed into her room. "I haven't thanked you for letting me use your bed."

He took a step toward her, and Samantha backed up to the door. "You're welcome. . . . I–I really don't think—"

"Don't run from me, Samantha. You have to know that wherever you go I'll just come after you."

Tears finally fell free from her eyes. "I can't . . . I can't be with you again only to have you leave me. I can't."

He reached out and cupped the side of her face,

brushing her tears away. "Do you know that every time you smile you take a little piece of my heart? That every time you look at me I fall in love with you all over again?"

Tears were spilling down her cheeks, and she was shaking her head. "Please. Please don't do this to me. Just go. Just go and leave me with what little we've had—"

"Have we really had so little?"

"Yes! Compared to what we *can* have!"

"Then tell me. Tell me what we can have."

"A home."

He rubbed his thumb along her bottom lip.

"A family."

He looked into her eyes.

"Each other."

He kissed her, sweet and long, and like a flower welcoming the sun she opened her arms and embraced him. She understood why she wasn't meant to have him. He was everything vital in the world, a power no woman could ever really call her own. She had to let him go.

"I love you, Max. But I won't try to hold you to a life that will only make you miserable . . ."

"How could life with you make me anything but happy?"

She sniffed. "I understand that sometimes in life you just have to let go . . ."

"And sometimes you have to hold on with both hands."

". . . and no matter if I never see you again, I want you to know that I'll never forget you, I'll always love you."

"And I'll always be here to remind you of it."

She looked up at him. "Did you say something?"

"I said, will you marry me, Samantha James?"

She blinked. "You did?"

He laughed and smoothed the frown from her forehead. "Funny, I always imagined a woman was supposed to smile when the man she loved asked her to be his wife."

"Did your grandmother talk you into this?"

"Nobody talked me into this, darlin'. I just came to some important conclusions."

"Such as?"

"Such as you drive me crazy in more ways than one, you're stubborn and scrappy, loving and loyal, you snore, dammit—I won't back down on that, and, frankly, I just can't go on living without you. Now, you say yes to my proposal or I'm gonna tie myself to your leg and you'll have to drag me around behind you for the rest of your life."

She laughed and threw her arms around his neck. He spun her in a circle and then tossed her onto the bed. "What say we celebrate?"

"No, no," she said, laughing and scrambling off the bed. "We set a date, right here and now. I'm not going to be like Camille and wait around for the rest of my life while you gallivant across the countryside catching outlaws."

He reached into his pocket and tossed her a flat metal object. She turned it over in her hand. It was a badge, and it read: *Cache County Sheriff.*

"There won't be any more gallivanting."

She circled the bed and wrapped her arms around his waist. "How about a December wedding?"

He gave her a disapproving look. "Too far off. How 'bout a next month wedding?"

"Next month?"

"Well, if a fella's gonna start living, he may as well start right away."

31

Max crept through the darkened house, past Ida's bedroom and toward Samantha's door. It was after three in the morning, and he hadn't slept a wink all night.

He tiptoed into Samantha's room and shut the door.

She was bundled up in the blankets of her bed, her rich brown hair fanned over the stark white of her pillow. The lamp on her bedside table was burning low, casting shadows across the walls, and he wondered briefly if she'd been waiting up for him.

He took off his pants and slipped naked beneath the covers, feeling her warmth envelop him. She sighed in her sleep and rolled toward him, draping her arms around his waist.

She was so beautiful in sleep that he was reluctant to wake her, but the need raging through his body for the past few weeks simply couldn't be denied any longer. He lowered his head and kissed her lightly.

She opened her eyes and smiled. "Couldn't wait one more night, hmmm?"

"It's either this or have a shaky, incredibly horny groom all over you tomorrow."

She pressed herself up against him. "If I have him all over me tonight . . . can I still have him all over me tomorrow?"

He laughed low in his throat, and the result was practically a growl. "Honey, you can have him whenever you like by just crooking your sweet little finger."

She raised her hands from the blankets and crooked her finger at him, and he gently pushed her back down on the mattress. "You're a wanton woman, Samantha James."

"Which makes me just perfect for this wantin' man," she said and giggled when he tickled her neck with his moustache.

He covered her mouth with his own and felt a slight tremor shake her and merge into his own body. He was hard and ready for her, as he had been for just about every day since he'd met her three months ago. And tomorrow she was going to be his legally, in the eyes of God and the world.

She broke away from their kiss. "Maybe we should go out to the barn."

"Are you kidding? I have yet to make love to you in a bed, Miss James. We aren't going anywhere."

He tried to resume their kiss, but she forestalled him. "But Ida. She's in the next room."

"Your aunt can go to hell—"

"What if she hears and comes barreling in here when we're . . . we're . . ."

"Copulatin'?" He grinned at her blush. "Don't worry, darlin'." He kissed her deeply. "I locked the door. And her broom ain't sharp enough to pick the lock."

Samantha did one more twirl in front of the full-length mirror, and the taffeta skirt of her wedding dress swished softly against her legs.

Brandon poked her head in the room. "Are you ready yet?"

Samantha inspected herself again, fingering the lace of her bodice. She couldn't remember the last time she'd been so nervous. Yes she could. It had been when she'd stood on the porch three weeks ago waiting for Max to make a decision about staying. "Can you give me a few more minutes, Brandon?"

Brandon laughed. "The guests at the church are bound to be getting restless. And if you take much longer Max is going to be over here pounding on your door, thinking you've left him at the altar. Now, come on. There's a surprise waiting out here for you."

"A surprise?" She took a deep breath, picked up her matching parasol, and followed Brandon out of the room.

Samantha paused in the hallway, not believing her eyes. Her father stood in the sitting room, dressed in a rich gray suit.

"Now, don't you cry, Samantha," Brandon warned. "Your face will get all puffy."

"Oh, Daddy," Samantha whispered as she flew into his arms. "How did you get here?"

"Barrett paid every penny of my stage fare. Said he wasn't about to marry a woman who wasn't given to him by her father. By the way"—his eyes turned misty—"you look wonderful."

"Daddy, you are the one who looks wonderful."

He gave her his arm and began to lead her toward the front door. "Have I told you recently how proud of you I am? Max Barrett is a lucky man, and he damn well better know it."

Samantha grinned, feeling such a burst of happiness and contentment she wanted to shout it to the world. They went out to the polished buggy Pete had loaned them and rode toward the small church on the outskirts of town.

She was met in the church alcove by Moriah, Ida, and Frances, who had become surprisingly open to the idea of the wedding since a date had been set.

She introduced them all to her father, and then Frances took her hands. "I've never seen my son so happy in his life, Samantha. You seem to have the uncanny ability to make him smile. I wish you both the best of luck."

Samantha stared at Frances Barrett's warm smile and again felt the urge to cry. "Thank you, Mrs. Barrett."

"Well, let's get this thing rolling," Moriah said. "It's almost lunch, and I'm half starved."

"Wait just one teensy little second!" called a voice from the front doorway. It was Camille. "I was not invited to this wedding, and I want to voice my loudest and most heated protest to that fact!"

The roomful of people groaned.

"Camille, honestly," Frances Barrett said. "Can't you simply cut your losses and move on?"

"Where there is a wedding there shall be me." A bright smile spread across her face. "And my newest beau."

Camille held out her arm, and Pete Holden edged into the doorway, a bright blush staining his cheeks. "She insisted on a grand entrance."

"And my dumpling never denies me anything," Camille said, beaming. "Do you, dumpling?"

The five other people in the alcove exchanged looks and started laughing—whether from relief or just plain joy, nobody was sure.

"Like I said," Moriah said, "let's get on with it!"

The doors to the meeting room opened, and

Samantha looked out upon the rows and rows of chairs that had been set up with a wide aisle down the center leading to the altar.

She was preceded by Brandon, who was serving as her maid of honor, and Grandmother Moriah, hobbling her way down the aisle, as her flower girl.

Her father lowered the veil over her face. "Ready to become Mrs. Barrett?"

She gripped his arm and nodded. They began their march down the aisle.

Max waited for her at the end, dressed in a dashing black suit and cravat. Her father placed her hand in her groom's.

"She's all yours, Barrett. Take good care of her or I'll set your hair on fire."

The ceremony began, but Samantha barely heard them. She was too intent on Max. Their hearts were joining together for all time, just like the hearts on the brooch she was wearing.

"I love you," Max said soundlessly.

She mouthed the words back, and, after being prompted twice, Max slipped the ring on her finger.

Samantha fought a giggle, realizing she couldn't even remember saying "I do."

Max lifted her veil, removing the last barrier that would ever stand between them. His lips touched hers, and a roar of applause went up from the onlookers.

As she turned toward the crowd her parasol caught Max on the side of the head. Stunned, she turned back to find him smiling.

"That's all right.," he told everyone. "I'm used to it."

If you enjoyed *Fan the Flame* you'll love *Kiley's Storm,* another delightful western historical romance by Suzanne Elizabeth—coming from HarperMonogram in February 1994.

AVAILABLE NOW

ONE GOOD MAN by Terri Herrington
From the author of *Her Father's Daughter*, comes a dramatic story of a woman who sets out to seduce and ruin the one good man she's ever found. Jilted and desperate for money, Clea Sands lets herself be bought by a woman who wants grounds to sue her wealthy husband for adultery. But when Clea falls in love with him, she realizes she can't possibly destroy his life—not for any price.

PRETTY BIRDS OF PASSAGE by Roslynn Griffith
Beautiful Aurelia Kincaid returned to Chicago from Italy nursing a broken heart, and ready to embark on a new career. Soon danger stalked Aurelia at every turn when a vicious murderer, mesmerized by her striking looks, decided she was his next victim—and he would preserve her beauty forever. As the threads of horror tightened, Aurelia reached out for the safety of one man's arms. But had she unwittingly fallen into the murderer's trap? A historical romance filled with intrigue and murder.

FAN THE FLAME by Suzanne Elizabeth
The romantic adventures of a feisty heroine who met her match in a fearless lawman. When Marshal Max Barrett arrived at the Washington Territory ranch to escort Samantha James to her aunt's house in Utah, little did he know what he was getting himself into.

A BED OF SPICES by Barbara Samuel
Set in Europe in 1348, a moving story of star-crossed lovers determined to let nothing come between them. "With her unique and lyrical style, Barbara Samuel touches every emotion. The quiet brilliance of her story lingered in my mind long after the book was closed."—Susan Wiggs, author of *The Mist and the Magic*.

THE WEDDING by Elizabeth Bevarly
A delightful and humorous romance in the tradition of the movie *Father of the Bride*. Emma Hammelmann and Taylor Rowan are getting married. But before wedding bells ring, Emma must confront not only the inevitable clash of their families but her own second thoughts—especially when she discovers that Taylor's best man is in love with her.

SWEET AMITY'S FIRE by Lee Scofield
The wonderful, heartwarming story of a mail-order bride and the husband who didn't order her. "Lee Scofield makes a delightful debut with this winning tale . . . *Sweet Amity's Fire* is sweet indeed."—Mary Jo Putney, bestselling author of *Thunder and Roses*.

COMING NEXT MONTH

LORD OF THE NIGHT by Susan Wiggs
Much loved historical romance author Susan Wiggs turns to the rich, sensual atmosphere of sixteenth-century Venice for another enthralling, unforgettable romance. "Susan Wiggs is truly magical."—Laura Kinsale, bestselling author of *Flowers from the Storm*.

CHOICES by Marie Ferrarella
The compelling story of a woman from a powerful political family who courageously gives up a loveless marriage and pursues her own dreams finding romance, heartbreak, and difficult choices along the way.

THE SECRET by Penelope Thomas
A long-buried secret overshadowed the love of an innocent governess and her master. Left with no family, Jessamy Lane agreed to move into Lord Wolfeburne's house and care for his young daughter. But when Jessamy suspected something sinister in his past, whom could she trust?

WILDCAT by Sharon Ihle
A fiery romance that brings the Old West back to life. When prim and proper Ann Marie Cannary went in search of her sister, Martha Jane, what she found instead was a hellion known as "Calamity Jane." Annie was powerless to change her sister's rough ways, but the small Dakota town of Deadwood changed Annie as she adapted to life in the Wild West and fell in love with a man who was full of surprises.

MURPHY'S RAINBOW by Carolyn Lampman
While traveling on the Oregon Trail, newly widowed Kate Murphy found herself stranded in a tiny town in Wyoming Territory. Handsome, enigmatic Jonathan Cantrell needed a housekeeper and nanny for his two sons. But living together in a small cabin on an isolated ranch soon became too close for comfort . . . and falling in love grew difficult to resist. Book I of the Cheyenne Trilogy.

TAME THE WIND by Katherine Kilgore
A sizzling story of forbidden love between a young Cherokee man and a Southern belle in antebellum Georgia. "Katherine Kilgore's passionate lovers and the struggles of the Cherokee nation are spellbinding. Pure enjoyment!"—Katherine Deauxville, bestselling author of *Daggers of Gold*.

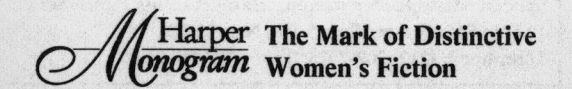

Harper Monogram The Mark of Distinctive Women's Fiction

ATTENTION: ORGANIZATIONS AND CORPORATIONS

Most HarperPaperbacks are available at special quantity discounts for bulk purchases for sales promotions, premiums, or fund-raising. For information, please call or write:
Special Markets Department, HarperCollins Publishers,
10 East 53rd Street, New York, N.Y. 10022.
Telephone: (212) 207-7528. Fax: (212) 207-7222.